Thaddeus Barcelona

Thaddeus Barcelona has a passion for plants. As curator of the North River City Botanical Gardens, he is living his dream. He also has discovered a life equation and feels no compunction about sharing it with anyone else, but uses it to understand the assorted personalities in his orbit.

Philosophers, musicians, artists, a plastic mannequin, and a dog named Anubis enter into the fray of a contentious mayoral election in the city of North River. Thaddeus, who has no political aspirations or interest, slowly gets sucked into the eclectic menagerie of characters and bizarre plots that unfold as two ballot measures play on the cultural divides of the city. Thaddeus finds humor in the absurd events surrounding the election as the mayor's older sister challenges him, and bumbling, religiously inspired kidnappings stoke the delusional musings of a few poor souls.

Other Books by
Rand Soler and Y.A Picker

The Sapience Threshold - *Rand Soler & Y.A. Picker*

The Origins Series
The Strings of Life - *Rand Soler & Y.A. Picker*
The Golden Seeds - *Rand Soler & Y.A. Picker*

Hach - *Y.A. Picker*

Beer for Breakfast - *Y.A. Picker*

Thaddeus Barcelona

by

Rand Soler

Published by Archean Enterprises, LLC

Archean Enterprises, LLC
16200 SW Pacific Hwy
Ste H #2055
Tigard, OR 97224

Author: **Rand Soler**

Content Consultant: **Y.A. Picker**

Cover Art: **ArcheanArt**

ISBNs:

Paperback: 978-1-958457-05-4

Ebook: 978-1-958457-04-7

The Life Equation

Thaddeus Barcelona was surprisingly average by most standard measurements. But standard measurements have difficulty defining the fringe. He had spun the roulette wheel of life many times, only to see his chips raked off the table. But he wasn't bothered. After all, life was more a game of chance than skill. A lesson he had learned early in life and was now reflecting upon again.

This particular day was not going as planned, but he would figure out how to cope with the change. Karen, his now ex-girlfriend, had packed her bags this morning and departed for locations unknown.

This sudden departure was not a complete surprise. Thaddeus had noticed, over the past several months, her growing anxiety over his prospects. They had discussed it often. Karen was fixated on him moving up to the next level, but he had a hard time visualizing what she meant. It was true he could make more money by "moving up," but then the shelves in his mental work pantry, where he stored delectable morsels, wouldn't be adequately stocked, and that was an important consideration. Each item in the pantry was an interesting, or maybe even fascinating, project he could pursue. He liked to pull them from the shelves as he pleased and indulge himself. So to him, moving up meant that many of these tasty treats would be replaced by unappetizing ones, like management meetings, budget planning, and increased personnel supervision.

He understood his concerns stemmed from a nebulous world outlook. But were you really living if you didn't have a personal philosophy, nebulous or not?

Thaddeus had observed subtle changes in Karen's life equation over their two-year relationship, and it was clear to him that she had rearranged its critical terms—not that Karen was aware she even had a life equation since Thaddeus was in sole possession of the formula. He accidentally stumbled upon his own life equation in community college and subsequently kept it to himself. But he tailored versions of it to each of his friends and acquaintances, attempting to understand what made them tick.

Horticulture was one of the ingredients making Thaddeus's life run smoothly. He learned gardening from his mom as a boy and never deviated from his fascination with plants and ecosystems. After all, a garden was just a miniature ecosystem.

Many of the subjects required in high school were unrelated to botany or ecology, and he easily lost interest. Of course, his lack of motivation reflected in his grades, and he was generally perceived as a poor student. Thaddeus was told more than once he had no aptitude for math, and he was encouraged to engage in only the minimal requirements. He was initially fine with this, but to his dismay, in his senior year, he realized one of his projects needed advanced statistical analysis. So, he spent several weeks reading books on probability and stochastic analysis. After absorbing what was needed, he stopped reading and started doing. Above all, Thaddeus was practical.

Community college treated him better, allowing him to focus on his primary obsession: horticulture.

One Friday afternoon during his second year, he was daydreaming on his way from a class and accidentally walked into a lecture on partial differential equations. Taking a seat in the back of the auditorium, he tried to comprehend the weird symbols on the screen as the instructor drew them on an overhead projector.

$$\frac{\partial^2 u}{\partial x^2} + \frac{\partial^2 u}{\partial y^2} + \frac{\partial^2 u}{\partial z^2} = 0$$

So $u(x,y,z)$ is a solution if it satisfies

remember $\frac{\partial u}{\partial x}$ is a partial derivative

Thaddeus always asked the same question of problems and unknowns: what part of this do I understand? The word *derivative* was his key to opening the door. He had learned about derivatives by measuring plant growth. If a plant grew five inches in five days, its growth rate—one inch per day—was the first derivative of its total displacement. Genius, he thought: the terms of the equation before him showed how a single factor changed in relation to three different inputs. It was at that moment he discovered his life equation. Thaddeus had heard enough from the professor. He cherished his general happiness and satisfaction with life, so he stopped paying attention to the rest of the lecture and composed his life equation.

Relationships, work, and shelter were the three variables in his life affecting his happiness. They were all important, but he valued work and relationships twice as much as shelter. He made the sum of the terms equal one since he liked the number. It represented wholeness and unity. It was a self-contained symbol of perfect balance.

$$(2)\frac{\partial h}{\partial r} + (2)\frac{\partial h}{\partial w} + \frac{\partial h}{\partial s} = 1$$

$$1 = unity = 1$$

h — happiness
r — relationships
w — work
s — shelter

When he first met Karen, she gave relationships a weight of three, with work, which she didn't like, and shelter, each getting a weight of one. Of course, this analysis was Thaddeus's assessment, not Karen's, since she didn't know about her life equation. Change is the only constant, though, and over the length of their relationship, she shifted her weightings, giving relationships a one and shelter a three. His 900-square-foot apartment didn't measure up to the new equation, and he had no desire to "move up." So, she left.

Above all, Thaddeus was practical. With Karen gone, he knew the negative change in relationships required a positive change in the work term of his life equation to maintain balance. His regular eight-hour days turned into ten- or even twelve-hour days. Working at the city's North River Botanical Gardens gave him a modest amount of spending money, an accumulating pension, healthcare, and enough left over to tuck away a bit into savings. With Karen gone and long hours at work, his savings portfolio was improving. All these things were good, but the job itself was the real jewel. Each day he cared for plants: watching their nutrition levels, controlling pests and diseases, ensuring proper amounts of shade and sun, and perfecting each plant's soil base.

Under his guiding eye, the gardens gained some international notoriety with an award last year. Several prominent botanists visited in the wake of the award. Thaddeus enjoyed talking with them; however, despite seeming very smart, he believed some of them lacked practical experience in running a botanical garden. But he kept this to himself and learned a few interesting facts about soil chemistry from the discussions.

Thaddeus's basement apartment was located close to the botanical gardens, so he walked to work each morning. The walking-distance factor was another reason he wasn't keen on "moving up." He had mentioned it once to Karen, but she scoffed at the idea that living close to his work was important, and he kept it to himself after that.

Every morning, he was the first to arrive at the gardens, and he went directly to the back of greenhouse 9, where an extra-large, red dog mat lay in the southeast corner. His upstairs neighbors had placed it in the trash outside after their dog, Theo, passed away. Thaddeus, remembering how much he liked Theo, took the mat in, cleaned it, and put it in the greenhouse to use during his morning meditations.

Starting the day with a fresh mind was one of Thaddeus's mantras in life. He sat cross-legged each morning on Theo's mat, emptied his thoughts, and let his mind drift into broad, quiet places. Sometimes he thought about Theo. A receptive mind was a creative mind, and creativity was the essence of horticulture.

Several months passed before he was ready to work on his life equation again. Although the botanical gardens were in tip-top shape, and Thaddeus believed the equation was balancing out to unity, there was some room for a positive change in the relationship term and a slight decline in the work term.

Experience told him that a new beginning was always a delicate time in his relationship cycles since small talk was not one of his notable talents. He didn't care who was on reality TV, nor did he take an interest in the latest movies or televised sports. Meeting intelligent women was difficult since Thaddeus avoided most social events, and though he occasionally enjoyed a cold beer, the late-night bar scene didn't agree with him.

His preference was toward a more passive approach to meeting women. He had observed in the past that the best relationships arose from unexpected encounters; you just had to be attentive to recognize the opportunity and not let it slip away. This sort of receptiveness required a clean, mindful outlook because the subtle signs were the ones that mattered most in this endeavor.

Weeks passed, and Thaddeus kept alert for those moments when energy patterns aligned and connections presented themselves. One of the components of his process was schedule modulation. Stick to the same schedule, go to the same places, and you will probably see the same faces, so Thaddeus mixed up his daily schedule and expanded the universe of places he visited. This particular Thursday, he started work at 5:00 a.m. and decided to take a 10:00 a.m. break to visit a funky little coffee shop just off Main Street called the Hot Rocks Café.

To get in the zone, he took a ten-minute meditation break before leaving on his three-block walk to the coffee house. Blue skies and 70 degrees made for a pleasant morning stroll. He hadn't been to Hot Rocks for a while. They roasted their beans on-site, so you were always sure to get a mouthful of deliciousness in every cup. He turned right on Main, walked past four storefronts, and pushed through the café's front door—walking into the present.

....

(Present)

Thaddeus looks around the room, taking in an eclectic array of wall hangings, sculptures, and other artwork. He recognizes two artists and then pauses to examine a new painting depicting a scene from the Oregon coast. The artist used black-and-white imagery in his work *Misty Day at Arcadia Beach*, creating a scene that perfectly captured an ocean fog rolling in over the tip of a coastal promontory. The land plunges into rough water and then disappears into the fog.

His gaze sweeps the room and stops at a mound of shinning black hair behind an open laptop. The woman raises her chin just a little, looking at Thaddeus with sparkling hazel-green eyes and flashing a smile his way. He returns it. She turns her attention back to her screen, and Thaddeus examines the electric jolt sweeping through his core. He heads to the counter to order and sees her glance in his direction from the corner of his eye. Events are unfolding rapidly, and Thaddeus recognizes the signs of a shifting cosmic alignment. He knows how delicate these moments are and that they can't be wasted.

When he picks up his coffee, he takes the long way to her table so she can follow his path through her peripheral vision. The small and delicate niceties of a first approach seem to jive with the energy waves he feels. A pause beside the table gives her a chance to look up before he speaks.

Thaddeus is not shy, but neither is he abrupt. "My name's Thaddeus. I was hoping I might join you for some coffee if it doesn't interrupt your work."

She lets her smile work its magic again before she speaks. "Well, Thaddeus, your timing is impeccable because I was just ready for a break. Have a seat." She motions to the chair next to her, not the one across the table. This is a good sign, and Thaddeus knows it. "My name is Melonie."

Thaddeus is electrified as another jolt of energy hits him. He thinks to himself that the cosmic wheel of fortune is spinning in his direction. He feels his life equation shifting yet again as the relationship term surges in a positive direction, and he wonders what kind of life equation Melonie has. Even though his equation has shifted, it still equals one and achieves unity.

Eighteen

Eighteen was a number of interest to Thaddeus. His basement apartment on Grove Avenue was an eighteen-minute walk from his office in the back of greenhouse 9 at the North River Botanical Gardens. Since he started seeing Melonie several months ago, he learned her third-floor condo was also an eighteen-minute walk from his office but in the opposite direction from his abode. He used the term office loosely to refer to a large desk his upstairs neighbors recently disposed of, which now occupied a small glass-walled room in the back of greenhouse 9. He found it a quiet and peaceful place to work, surrounded by all manner of plants in various stages of growth.

The more Thaddeus contemplated the number eighteen, the more intrigued he became. The fact that it was a multiple of nine added a certain spice to his mental deliberations, nine being such an auspicious number itself. People who like reading the Bible are fond of pointing out that Jesus expired in the ninth hour of his ordeal, and he then appeared nine times to his disciples after the resurrection. Abram was ninety-nine when he established his covenant with God and changed his name to Abraham.

In the Hindu tradition, nine is considered a complete, perfect, and divine number since it represents the end of a cycle in the decimal system. The Chinese see it as a lucky number symbolic of completeness, and it is similar in pronunciation to the word meaning everlasting. Thaddeus was so impressed with this fact that he gave Melonie nine roses on her birthday just a month ago.

Many people were clearly in on the nine action, and while Thaddeus didn't fully understand all the nuances, he still liked the number. Four nines gave him thirty-six, the number of minutes needed to walk to Melonie's condo from his basement apartment. After a month of trekking back and forth to visit at all hours of the night and day, he recognized a change was needed.

Thaddeus could drive, but he had never owned a car. When he wanted to get out of town, he rented one, a simple alternative. The system had worked fine for years, but he couldn't rent a car whenever he wanted to zip over to Melonie's. He had no desire to own a car and take on the expenses and headaches of maintaining a vehicle. But while reading the news one day, an idea presented itself. The article was about an influx of electric scooters in big cities. The piece mainly focused on the nuisance created by scooters lying around, blocking the sidewalks and cluttering the streets while waiting for riders, as well as the scooter operator's lousy road manners. But all Thaddeus saw was an opportunity.

After careful research, he settled on a Dorsal Eighteen MAX. It could travel up to forty miles on a single charge, and interestingly it cruised at a top speed of eighteen miles per hour. Melonie's condo was exactly two miles from Thaddeus's apartment, and the Dorsal Eighteen could make the trip in nine minutes on average, allowing for traffic lights. He once made it in six minutes by hitting all the lights just right and taking advantage of a final three-block downhill section where gravity offered some additional speed. The scooter was a handy enhancement to his simple lifestyle, and Melonie confided how he looked a bit dashing in his helmet with his brown ponytail flying in the wind.

He checked his phone: five o'clock. Melonie would be dropping by soon. They planned to catch a beer by the river at the Pearl Bridge Bar before walking back to her place. It was a spectacular autumn day. The kind of day most people live for, with crisp air, blue skies, and warm sunshine to light up all the dazzling maples in their autumn colors. He had taken the Dorsal Eighteen to work that morning, and it was nestled into the far corner of his office, hooked into a charger.

At precisely eighteen minutes after five, he looked up. Melonie was coming down the greenhouse's central aisle between tables of azaleas and several rows of experimental Japanese maples. She flashed him the same smile that won him over when he first saw her at the Hot Rocks Café. He felt giddy as always.

Melonie described herself as Afro-Hispano-Caribbean with a touch of Italian. All Thaddeus knew was her sparkling hazel-green eyes and radiant smile made her the most desirable woman he had ever seen. But as the relationship grew, he found more beauty within. They both vibrated on the same frequency, which he referred to as wavelength 9.

·········

(Present)

He waves to her and reaches into the top right desk drawer, retrieving two neatly rolled joints, and slips them into the inner pocket of his vest. Thaddeus is and always has been a gardener. Horticulture is his passion, and his job at the botanical gardens is as close to a dream position as he can imagine.

Several years ago, the legalization of recreational cannabis made his life easier, letting him work more openly on one of his long-term hobbies, developing the perfect strain of marijuana. Last year he filed for a patent on a custom-developed strain he called Gaia Gold Eighteen. It was in the eighteenth generation of this plant when he believed perfection had been narrowly obtained. Thaddeus paid to have the genome mapped for a patent application, and he is now pondering where to take his project in the future.

Thaddeus and Melonie wander through the gardens toward the northwest corner of the property. There, along the river, sits a huge flat-topped granite bolder. He considers it his private seat on the riverfront stage. It is only accessible via the botanical gardens and, even then, off the beaten path.

Thaddeus exhales a long cloud of smoke as they sit on the boulder, and he listens to Melonie, watching her animated description of the riverfront restoration project she manages.

Like in many towns, the river started as a natural asset for industrial exploitation. Slightly upriver from the botanical gardens, mills were built around the waterfalls in the mid-1800s. Manufacturing enterprises came and went using natural waterpower to drive their businesses. A small electric power generation station still operates beside the falls. For over a hundred years, businesses developed along the riverbanks, and every one of them dumped their waste in the river to save money on disposal.

Eventually, in 1972, the Clean Water Act forced manufacturers to start cleaning up their operations and stop wantonly dumping pollutants into the country's waterways. From this initial outcry of public disgust grew the seeds of environmental consciousness and a renewed interest in maintaining natural resources in a usable but sustainable way. Earth science programs at major universities started turning out ecologists, and conservation groups became popular. Melonie grew up in this world, so it was not wholly surprising when she decided to study environmental sciences as an undergrad and later pursued a PhD in ecology.

Melonie gestures slightly upriver from their rock. "First we'll restore the native riparian habitats along both riverbanks for a mile upstream. Then we'll replant native shrubs, grasses, and small trees along the banks so most areas will have a large green boundary between the city and the river. The open field directly across from us will become a small arboretum. Once the green borders are in place, the habitats for amphibians, red-legged frogs, water birds, weasels, and even otters will improve. We are combining this with an effort to eliminate seventy percent of the current waste discharge into the river so native fish species can also thrive."

Thaddeus listens intently, loving the enthusiasm in her voice when she gets wired up on ecological restorations.

"A little farther upstream," she says, "where the sandstone hills rise away from the river, we'll let the grasslands and savanna oaks return. It's going to be beautiful, Thaddeus."

He takes another toke and marvels at the goodness of his current situation. His life equation is balancing out most satisfactorily. Sunshine streams over his left shoulder, and red, orange, and yellow leaves swirl across the grassy field on the other side of the river. They both sit back in silence and let the warm late-autumn afternoon mingle and merge with the Gaia Gold. After a time, they head west out of the botanical gardens through an obscure gate in the border fence. Thaddeus is one of the few people with a key to this gate. From there, it's just a brief walk along the riverbank to the Pearl Bridge Bar. Clear, dark water swirls along the water's edge, forming intricate fractal patterns. He points them out to Melonie, who always delights in the recursive but strangely artistic beauty of such things.

The two enjoy Boneyard IPAs on the Pearl's front patio, listening to the background drone of rush-hour traffic crossing the river and watching kayakers out for their evening exercise.

Thirty minutes later, they turn the corner onto Elm Street, just half a block from Melonie's condo building. Their conversation drifts to bees, a subject near and dear to Thaddeus's heart. "No bees, no garden" is one of his quotes. Melonie recently learned that a neighbor on her floor, Grant, kept beehives on the building's roof. Evidently, the condo homeowners association approved the arrangement several years ago. Thaddeus contemplates this information since he has been considering establishing several beehives in the botanical gardens at strategic locations.

He glances up the street. "You have a protester outside your condo. What the heck is that about?"

"Oh," she replies, "that's Maggie, or Mad Maggie, as Grant says."

Thaddeus is now close enough to read the poster bobbing on a stick over her head. *Free the Bees*, the sign says with the word *Free* in bright red. Maggie looks to be in her early sixties, with a thick, tight braid of gray hair down her back. She is under five feet tall and appears fit. A long tartan skirt hangs down to her ankles, and she's wearing a bright yellow shirt with the graphic design of a bee on the back over the words *Bee Good!* Her outfit is topped off with a pair of red Converse high tops.

Melonie waves to her, shouting, "Maggie, good to see you today."

Maggie puts her sign down and walks over to give Melonie a big hug. "Is this the young man you told me about?" She asks while giving Thaddeus a wink from one of her twinkling blue eyes.

"He is indeed, Maggie."

"Well, young man, it's good to finally meet you. I attend all of the neighborhood meetings on the river restoration project, and I want you to know your girlfriend is one smart cookie."

Thaddeus smiles and eyes the protest sign again.

Now standing behind Maggie, Melonie shakes her head no for Thaddeus to see. "You don't have to tell me, Maggie. I already know it." He refrains from asking about the sign.

Melonie steps back to his side and locks arms with him. "We need to run upstairs and get dinner going, Maggie. Good luck with the protest."

"You two kids have a great evening," she says before whirling around to retrieve her sign and get back to work.

"What's that all about?" Thaddeus asks.

Melonie glances over her shoulder as the lobby door shuts, then speaks in a slightly muted tone to Thaddeus. "Maggie believes bees shouldn't be kept in artificial hives. She describes herself as advocating for the free-range bee movement—she wants all her buzzing friends back in hollowed-out trees and such. Somehow, she got wind of Grant's activities on the roof, so she's been protesting outside our building from time to time. But Grant's a good guy. He takes the whole thing well. The other day he took some folding chairs out and sat with Maggie for an hour, trying to convince her that the bees on the roof come and go as they please and don't mind living in his hives. She thanked him for the explanation and for the cold soda he brought her but stuck firmly to her theory that free-ranging involves not only where the bees go but also where they live."

"So," says Thaddeus, "you accidentally told her about Grant's bees."

Melonie sighs and gives him a look to make him melt. It works, and he drops the subject.

They exit the elevator just as Grant is leaving his condo.

"Grant, wait!" Melonie hollers. Grant stops and turns. "Grant, this is Thaddeus, and he's interested in your bees."

"Really. I was just heading up to see them." Grant strides back down the hallway to shake Thaddeus's hand.

Melonie stops at her front door and tells Thaddeus to go with Grant and have a look. She disappears inside, and the two guys hop on the service elevator. Thaddeus glances at the control panel and notices the building has eighteen floors when he counts the roof service exit. He ponders this and files it away with the rest of his number-eighteen information. The elevator deposits them on a small landing with a heavy gray metal door off to the right, close to a stairwell. The lock beeps after Grant punches in a code, then he opens the door, letting in bright sunshine. Thaddeus pauses before exiting and takes in a view of the city illuminated by the late afternoon sun, a landscape of brilliant light and deep shadows.

Grant strides over to the rooftop's south side, where white hives are neatly arranged about three feet off a safety wall.

"Nine hives," says Thaddeus. "That is an auspicious number, my friend."

"It is indeed, and it's not random. I place some stock in numbers, and nine hives bring completeness to the venture."

Thaddeus nods and turns his attention to the frenzied activity and humming coming from the hives. At the same time, Grant launches into a fascinating monologue about how he maintains the hives and why they are beneficial to the environment. Grant is preaching to the choir, but Thaddeus listens and files away some details for his own bee venture at the botanical gardens. Thaddeus has an amazing memory, except for the items he deliberately forgets. He is keen on keeping his memory banks filled with useful information and not allowing too much clutter.

At a pause in the conversation, Thaddeus asks Grant what his day job is.

Grant looks up from his task of picking up debris around the hives. "I work over at the New Amsterdam, at Main and Fifth. In fact, I own it."

Thaddeus is familiar with the New Amsterdam cannabis shop, and as the mental wheels turn, his mind shifts focus from bees to Gaia Gold. "So, you also own the cannabis greenhouse on the west side of the Pearl Street Bridge?" He had read in a local magazine article that the shop and greenhouse were owned by the same person and wanted to confirm the information before proceeding.

"That's me," replies Grant with a smile. "Production and retail."

This moment is one of those rare opportunities for Thaddeus when various metaphysical vibrations coalesce into a single harmonious waveform. In a split second, he has a prescient vision of a path materializing into the future. He runs through a dozen ways to push the go button and make things happen, but in the end, he decides to let direct action speak for itself. He reaches into his vest pocket, pulls out a perfectly rolled joint of Gaia Gold, lights up, and offers it to Grant.

Grant takes several slow, relaxed drags and examines the joint while he rolls it slowly between his fingers. He says nothing but wanders over to the west wall and pauses to take in the remains of the day. After a few minutes, he asks, "Where did you get this?"

"I grew it. It's the end result of eighteen generations of cultivation. I recently got a genetic patent on it."

"I've never sampled anything like it," Grant murmurs. "It actually smokes like luxurious tobacco, with a hint of moistness, and it has a fabulous mellow kick to it. This is intensely good weed."

"It's more than just genetics," continues Thaddeus. "The growing and drying processes are very tightly controlled."

Grant takes another toke, thinks for a moment, then continues. "Melonie tells me you're the botanist for the North River Botanical Gardens. Would you consider doing some consulting on the side for me at the production greenhouse? I'm sure we could work out a royalty agreement on the patent and get this product to market. Tell me again, what do you call it?"

"Gaia Gold. I think the letters GG could be fashioned into quite a marketable logo," says Thaddeus as Grant hands the joint back to him. "I'm in. Let's seal up a contract and get moving."

Thaddeus now realizes the future path for his creation. No need to *flounder in the bushes*, he thinks. *The key to life is action.*

"I'll have something by early afternoon tomorrow," says Grant.

Thaddeus speaks slowly with a smile on his face: "About eighteen hours from now sounds like a grand starting point for a new venture."

They both stand in silence, admiring the colors in the western sky. Thaddeus understands his life equation has just shifted, but he needs more time to contemplate the new balance.

Delusional Humanism

The message from Cranstone was clear: he wanted to meet before the end of the week. Thaddeus was familiar with Cranstone's life equation and didn't ask any questions. He simply set up a 5:30 p.m. rendezvous at the Pearl Bridge Bar for Thursday.

Now Thursday afternoon had arrived, and Thaddeus was hurrying across the North River Botanical Gardens grounds toward the northwest corner. From there, he slipped through the gate and made his way along the riverbank in the direction of the bar. The sky was a glorious blue, and the sweet fertile smell of the river hung in the air.

He checked his watch as he scurried past the Pearl and along the walkway beneath the bridge. He had allowed for an extra thirty minutes to do a quick check on the New Amsterdam greenhouse. His recent business arrangement with Grant had him frequenting the greenhouse since he was licensing his patented Gaia Gold strain to New Amsterdam Enterprises for the product's first commercial test. Grant had set out a quarter of the available greenhouse space for this test, and Thaddeus was determined to make it a success.

Immediately after passing the Pearl Bridge, he turned left up a flight of stairs leading to street level. At the top, he took a half-block walk to his right, down River Road, which landed him at the front door of the greenhouse. Thaddeus punched his personal code into the keypad and heard the familiar sharp click as the door unlocked.

He shut the door behind him and looked around for Grant, who had said he would be on site this afternoon. Grant's cannabis retail shop, the New Amsterdam, was only five blocks away, so he was either in the back or on his way. Thaddeus strolled toward the southwest corner of the building, passing through another door into the Gaia Gold quadrant. Thin plexiglass walls sealed this section off from the others. Normally the growing area of the greenhouse was wide open from front to back. But Thaddeus had convinced Grant to temporarily wall off this section to provide tighter environmental controls and optimal growing conditions for this first crop.

He first walked the rows, visually inspecting the plants but finding no real cause for concern. Last week he ran spot chemical analyses on several plant samples to ensure the current nutrient feed was having its desired effect. The results confirmed they were on target for a good batch. He had just pulled off a random leaf and was inspecting it when Grant walked in.

"How is it looking, Thaddeus?"

Thaddeus ripped the leaf in two and held it up to the light to inspect its color and hue, paying particular attention to the ripped edge where light refracted through rough, thin fragments of moist, freshly exposed plant tissue. He crushed a portion of the leaf between his thumb and forefinger, examined the residue, and took a slow sniff. Finally, he dabbed some residue on the tip of his tongue.

"I like it, Grant. I think we have a great crop on the way. I would suggest starting the light fifteen minutes earlier in the morning and increasing the humidity by five percent."

"Done," replied Grant. "I've started preparing some advertising, hyping the mellowness of Gaia Gold. Drop by the retail shop in the next day or two and have a look. I think you'll like the logo. If you have some time now, come on back to the tasting room, and we can talk about the packaging."

"I will absolutely come by tomorrow after work on my way over to Melonie's. But I can't hang out and have a smoke right now. I need to be at the Pearl in a couple of minutes. Cranstone has something urgent to discuss."

Grant rolled his eyes. "Is he still yammering on about his delusional humanism theory?"

"I can only suspect so. It's not as crazy as it sounds, you know. But he can't seem to gain much traction from his academic peers."

Cranstone Fletcher had three PhDs in philosophy, sociology, and psychology. He held a tenured position at North River State University, but Thaddeus had first met him by accident when he attended community college. Thaddeus had shown up in the main lecture hall on a Wednesday afternoon, anticipating an exciting talk on symbiotic gardening techniques. He arrived at four o'clock on the nose, but in his usual style, on the wrong day. It turned out Cranstone was doing eight weekly lectures on "the role of social psychology in modern society." Thaddeus had no interest in social psychology. But he considered this accidental opportunity nonrandom and felt the best course of action was to let fate play out and listen. During this lecture, he was first exposed to Cranstone's theory on delusional humanism.

The term humanism emphasized the primary importance of human, rather than divine, influences in achieving personal fulfillment and social harmony. But Cranstone possessed a cynical streak, as overly brilliant people sometimes do, and he couldn't rationalize modern society's actions to include critical thinking and good judgment.

His cynicism was further stoked and aggravated by his mentor, whom he referred to only as the Doctor. He had remarked to Thaddeus once that the Doctor often compared life to the act of eating. "Life comes in through the mouth and leaves through the anus" was one of his sayings. And another time, in a somewhat prescient moment, he predicted he would die by passing out of his own asshole. As fate would have it, he died bleeding out when a massive hemorrhoid burst while he sat on the toilet. Evidently, he was reading Søren Kierkegaard's magnum opus, Either/Or, at the time of his passing. He left the book neatly laid on a small table beside the toilet with a carefully placed bookmark on which he scribbled a final note to Cranstone. Thaddeus had asked before, but Cranstone would never discuss the note's contents.

After much thinking and several doctorate degrees, Cranstone came to certain conclusions regarding the human condition. The first of these resulted from his observation that humans devoted very little of their mental power to rational thought. Neuroscience backed him up by determining that most of the brain's energy went to subconscious processes, not conscious contemplation. As he further observed, the small bit of effort directed toward conscious thinking included very little rational thought. Instead, most people used their minds to rearrange facts into stories supporting their emotional beliefs, often discarding troublesome bits of factual data and only retaining what confirmed their preconceived biases.

He saw people's propensity to hold deep beliefs, which were false and clearly contradicted by facts, as psychotic delusions prohibiting them from distinguishing real from unreal.

Cranstone's concept of delusional humanism viewed society as being deeply influenced by the majority's willingness to accept delusion over reality. In his opinion, society's misguided direction stemmed from people's inability to apply rational planning and critical thinking to their daily problem-solving.

Thaddeus was not a grand philosopher; nonetheless, he was impressed with Cranstone's first lecture and ended up attending the entire series. He also found that Cranstone was not averse to burning a joint after his lectures and discussing the nitty-gritty of his worldviews. Thaddeus had enjoyed these conversations and kept in contact with Cranstone over the years, although in person, he always referred to him as "Professor," rarely using his first name.

Thaddeus arrived at the Pearl on time and saw the Professor sitting at his favorite table in the corner. The table was empty except for the Professor's phone. Thaddeus held up two fingers, and Cranstone vigorously nodded. He returned two minutes later with Boneyard IPAs in each hand. A bit of golden-colored beer glinted in the sunlight and slopped over the top of one glass as he placed them on the table.

"Professor, good to see you again." Thaddeus sat down and slid a small thin box across the table. The Professor nodded a thank-you and slipped the box containing four perfectly rolled Gaia Golds into his inner vest pocket. Cranstone was a longtime enthusiast of Thaddeus's cannabis cultivation project. "How's the book coming?"

Cranstone had been working on this latest book for a year now, and Thaddeus figured it must be near completion. "It's coming along nicely. I've almost finished the final section on the Rumpers and hypnotic mass hysteria." Thaddeus shook his head knowingly.

The Professor had developed a theory about large-scale delusional events and how they affect society. His mention of 'Rumpers' referenced events from years ago when the sitting, single-term president, Daniel Rump, tried to convince the world he won an election after all vote counts and recounts affirmed he was the loser. Cranstone didn't care one whit about politics from a partisan perspective, but he was fascinated by how the events of that election supported his case for delusional humanism as a valid social philosophy.

The facts of the case were clear. President Rump lost the popular vote by twenty million, and his opponent received 351 electoral votes, leaving Rump with only 187. A mere four years earlier, President-elect Rump described this type of margin as a landslide. But in the wake of his stunning and decisive defeat, Rump still insisted he won the election. This declaration was no real surprise to anyone who followed Rump's career, but the fact that he convinced fifty million followers he had won was staggering.

Cranstone reflected on these events for several years before he introduced his theory of hypnotic mass hysteria. Hypnotic refers to how individuals become subconsciously receptive to ideas from another individual. Mass indicates the large number of people affected, and hysteria characterizes an uncontrolled outburst of irrational behavior. His treatment of the subject was not about attacking Rump but rather about investigating how he had so skillfully executed a strategy engaging fifty million voters in a delusional fantasy.

The Professor had first explained his thinking to Thaddeus in the following terms. "It harkens back to the craft of the master hypnotist. Using repetitive motions or sounds, he creates an atmosphere of well-being and lures his subject into a mental state where they are open to his suggestions. One trick the master hypnotist uses is to fashion suggestions that don't override his subject's belief system—instead, he plays on that belief system to make the suggestions seem reasonable. How else could a hypnotist convince someone to stand on one foot and act like a chicken?

"So the question is, how do you carry out this trick on fifty million people? The first step is you create a believable alternate reality. Remember, despite the nasty virus circulating across the country, Rump continued to hold in-person rallies with thousands of people. This particular trick imparted a sense of overwhelming support. His followers believed the majority of voters were strongly on their side. By the time the election rolled around, Rumpers believed it impossible for them to lose.

"Step two was a repetitive motion to lull them into a state of receptive hypnosis. This stage was accomplished with two simple words: voter fraud. For a year before the election, his supporters were inundated daily with the false notion that voter fraud was a viable and imminent threat. Rump was a master at rhythmically dangling the words back and forth in his communications until his flock reverted to believing what was false was really true. With ample deep conditioning, the Rumpers were wide open to Rump's assertion he won the election, despite overwhelming and incontrovertible evidence pointing to his loss. I believe this to be a classic example of hypnotic mass hysteria. The Rumpers were effectively hypnotized by a master grifter. The mass hypnosis created a collective delusion and resulted in a hysterical outpouring of irrational behavior."

Thaddeus wasn't sure about the theory, but he did remember talking to Rump supporters after the election, trying to understand their claim that their man had won. But Thaddeus didn't like talking politics and was searching for a way to veer from going down a rabbit hole. "I'm glad to hear you're wrapping things up with the book. When do you think it will go to publication?"

"Soon, Thaddeus. I have a feeling this may be the key to catapulting delusional humanism into the academic forefront. I have high hopes."

Thaddeus liked the Professor and had high hopes also; he wanted to see the Professor achieve one of his lifelong goals. But despite the Professor's sharp mind, Thaddeus worried when he sometimes slipped into his own delusions. Thaddeus had once looked up Cranstone Fletcher in Wikipedia and found a glowing article describing him as the "father of modern delusional humanism." This description was a little too optimistic to have been written by anyone other than the Professor himself.

Thaddeus was relieved as the conversation shifted in an unexpected direction. "Well, I have some good news to share, Thaddeus." Cranstone paused and took a sip of beer. "Wedding nuptials are in my near future."

Thaddeus was surprised. The Professor was in his mid-sixties, and as far as Thaddeus knew, he had only been married once to a woman named Barbara, whom he always referred to as *the Barb*. It was a short-lived affair, ending in divorce when the Barb ran off with a circus trapeze artist named Angelina. In the Professor's own words, their marriage was a "match challenged by divergent biological imperatives." Sometimes he would simply say he had been "stung by the Barb."

"Congratulations, Professor," Thaddeus said while raising his glass in a toast. "This is an excellent piece of news. Who is the lucky lady?"

"You probably don't know her, Thaddeus. She is an enticing enchantress by the name of Maggie Harper."

Thaddeus paused. "Are we talking about Maggie of 'free the bees' fame?"

Cranstone was a bit surprised. "Well, yes... one and the same. I assume you have made her acquaintance, then."

"I have, Professor. Not long ago, she was protesting in front of my girlfriend's condo building. It seems that Grant is one of Melonie's neighbors, and he has a side hobby of keeping beehives on the roof."

The Professor seemed a bit unsettled, shifted in his seat, and gazed out the window overlooking the North River for a moment. "Yes, she is a little upset with Grant. In fact, she wanted me to stop shopping at the New Amsterdam, but I quite like Grant and keep it to myself now when I need to restock. Maggie is discreet and doesn't inquire as to the origins of my purchases. But I think she will be quite pleased with your generous gift today. She has never actually sampled the magnificence of Gaia Gold."

"Thanks for the compliment, Professor. Give her my regards and tell her I am thrilled at the wedding news. Do you have a date?"

"Actually, Thaddeus, that's what I'm here to talk to you about this afternoon. Maggie and I would like to be married in the rose garden gazebo at the botanical gardens. I was hoping you might help me with those arrangements. What, with you being the horticultural celebrity of the town, I'm sure you carry some sway."

Thaddeus smiled. "I don't know about sway or horticultural celebrity, but I can certainly fix you up with your wedding location. You send me the date you want, and if it is not already taken, I will book you in."

"Excellent," said Cranstone. "We have already decided that our first choice is March twentieth of next spring. Let me write a deposit check out for you now."

Thaddeus held up his palm. "Can't do, Professor. Consider it my treat as a wedding gift to you and Maggie."

Cranstone thanked Thaddeus with another clink of the glasses. He was silent for a moment, and Thaddeus detected a bit of tension—he was reasonably adept at picking up body language and subtle social cues. The Professor's voice was pitched slightly too high as he started in on an unexpected conversational tangent. "I saw in the paper last month that there have been some mysterious thefts of beehives. I hope the North River Botanical Gardens hasn't been affected. A beehive is a very odd sort of thing to steal."

"Actually, someone is removing frames from the medium supers in the beehives and taking off with both the honey and the bees. Never enough to destroy the hive but damaging nonetheless. It all happened last August at the height of the honey harvest season. We've only started with beehives at the gardens and won't be in full operation until next spring, so we haven't had any problems.

"An unfortunate problem," said the Professor, and then he went silent again.

Thaddeus slowly sipped his beer and pondered. The fact that Cranstone would bring the subject up was unusual since he was never one to get excited about horticultural matters. But Cranstone's relationship with Maggie raised the specter of undivulged knowledge. The Professor certainly knew more than he was saying, and Thaddeus was piecing together parts of the mysterious bee-theft puzzle. He said nothing and redirected the conversation until they finished their beers and parted ways.

After the Professor left, Thaddeus entered a calendar note on his phone, reminding himself to book the rose garden gazebo. He then sat for a few minutes and thought a bit more about the beehive thefts. His beehive project was an important part of the garden's sustainability project, and he may need to take some additional precautions to ensure the safety of his hives. He filed that thought away since they were more in the planning-and-development stage than in full-blown operational mode.

The Professor's life equation was shifting, and Thaddeus could feel it. "Food for thought," he muttered to himself as he made his way over to Melonie's. She would be home from work soon, and he wanted to discuss his suspicions with her. She would also be delighted at the upcoming wedding since she was quite fond of Maggie.

Mad Maggie

Spring was well underway in North River, and Thaddeus was spending extra time each day at the botanical gardens, working to establish beehives at several locations around the grounds. His plan focused on strategically placing the hives in areas where the bees could pollinate a variety of flowering plants and ornamental fruit trees. Still, the hives also had to be positioned away from the public. Grant, because of his beekeeping knowledge, was an unpaid consultant on this work.

This particular morning, they were near the northeast corner of the gardens. Cranstone and Maggie had been wed a month before, and Grant reminisced a bit over the chaotic March wedding while Thaddeus used white chalk powder and stakes with orange tops to mark a spot for the second hive location. The wedding ceremony was one Thaddeus would not easily forget.

The event was held in the Victorian gazebo at the center of the rose garden. The decorative wood structure with white columns and a dark green tin roof sat gracefully among some of the city's most glorious roses. It was spacious enough for immediate family and a few more, and chairs to accommodate the rest of the guests lined the grass lawn in front of the gazebo.

To the right of the structure was a small stage for the band. Maggie had insisted on Jill Jammin for her music and entertainment. Thaddeus was only vaguely familiar with Jill, but she had local cult status, and both Maggie and Melonie were fans. Jill had gained fame several years prior from her vivid and enthusiastic protest songs during the presidency of Daniel Rump.

Rump was in his active wall-building stage when she got her first boost to stardom. Walls, both real and imaginary, were being constructed in a public relations effort to appease his core followers. The RAG movement (Return America to Greatness) was in full swing, providing cover for his generally psychotic supporters, whose visions of history tactfully ignored the country's origin as a nation of immigrants.

Jill's ire peaked when her boyfriend, Pablo-Raul, a Honduran Muslim, went home for a three-month visit with family and found he couldn't get back into the country. Jill assembled her band and took to the streets with daily protest concerts. Thaddeus had only heard them play once, and he was impressed with the Janice Joplin–like quality of Jill's voice. The music itself defied placement in any particular genre, perhaps because of the unconventional spirits in the three-piece ensemble.

Jill's percussionist was Harpie, who specialized in bongos and other hand drums, although he occasionally kept the beat rolling with spoons or other assorted instruments. At one time, he would bring a stringless old wooden bass to their shows, mount it on a homemade two-by-four frame, and pound out a rhythm using his fingertips and the heel of his hand. The third member was Flower, who played all varieties of flutes and occasionally a harmonica.

Jill was the front person with a signature hot-pink Fender Strat. Thaddeus recalled she could spontaneously wander off on some amazing lead solos when she had a mind to. She and Flower could go on for hours, echoing licks back and forth, while Harpie madly laid down a beat in the background. Jill usually kept the tips of her hair dyed pink to match the guitar.

They were in fine form on the day of the wedding. Harpie was firmly back on the bongos, with no spoons, and his head was shaven and waxed, and it glared in the sun. The day was mildly warm, but by midceremony, sweat rolled down the smooth black skin of his head. Flower had her hair done in dreadlocks, and although Jill usually only dyed her hair tips to match her guitar, her head had gone full pink for the wedding.

Their performance included one of Jill's signature protest pieces, "Flight of the Android Bees." Before the wedding, Melonie had explained to Thaddeus that it was an instrumental reenactment of a swarm of android bees chasing President Rump across the White House lawn. Thaddeus's interest peaked.

As Thaddeus and Grant reminisced, Thaddeus fondly recalled the entire scene.

·········

(Present action)

Jill's music, slated for an interlude just before the final vows, starts slow and mellow with Harpie's beat depicting a morning stroll across the presidential lawn. Flower weaves a springlike flute melody around the bongos, growing louder as the bees approach the White House grounds. In the meantime, Jill makes her guitar gently hum and buzz in weird ways as the android bees take pleasure in floating here and there, looking for flowers.

About midway through, Harpie picks up the pace, and Flower's flute flutters across some disharmonious rifts as Rump bulldozes across a flower bed, crushing daffodils and budding tulips. The bees swerve, moving toward the intrusion, and Jill slowly raises the volume on her guitar. Soon Rump realizes the bees are pursuing him, and Harpie's beat gets frantic as the president lumbers into a run.

The bees, maddened to a fever pitch at the spectacle of crushed flowers, pick up the attack. Jill shifts to full volume, causing several guests near the amplifier to fall out of their seats onto the grass. Flower has taken to random high-pitch squeaks, simulating Rump's fear, when suddenly Jill charges toward the amp with her guitar, producing an exquisite bit of earsplitting feedback as the bees reach Rump and sting him in the butt.

By this time, Maggie has abandoned the gazebo and is dancing wildly in the aisle between the chairs, jabbing her right index finger into the air and screaming, "Sting him again, sting him again."

Jill obliges by repeatedly leaping around the amp, creating four more bursts of manic feedback, like someone had amplified the sound of a chicken being struck by lightning.

The audience's reaction is mixed. Some of the original fallen are still rolling around on the grass. Others have frozen smiles on their faces, and a few are in tears. Cranstone, who reacts poorly to loud, unexpected noises, has collapsed onto his knees with his hands over his ears.

Rowland, the Buddhist monk presiding over the ceremony, maintains a benign smile as he pats Cranstone's back. From his second-row seat, Thaddeus sees Rowland's lips moving and assumes he is trying to comfort Cranstone, but Thaddeus hears nothing over the acoustic melee. Melonie is tapping her foot, enjoying the show.

The music drops off into discordant shuffling sounds made by the secret service agents as they drag Rump inside. It ends with a soft, happy buzz from Jill's guitar when the bees depart and return to their spaceship-shaped hive.

Some weddings generate more memories than others.

....

Grant and Thaddeus were still laughing about the android bees when the buzzer on his belt went off, indicating someone had opened the bee enclosure near the gardens' southwest edge. The hive was newly established—no one should have been in there. Thaddeus had installed an alarm due to the recent rash of unexplained beehive thefts around the city. The modus operandi was always the same: someone removed frames from the medium supers and escaped with the honey and the bees.

Thaddeus told Grant to carry on, and he took off at a run toward greenhouse 9. There, plugged into a wall charger, sat his Dorsal Eighteen MAX. He entered the greenhouse, grabbed his scooter, and powered down the center aisle and out the open front door. He forgot his helmet, so his hair waved out behind him like a flag. He zipped across the grounds and onto the West Fence Service Road, speeding toward the beehive enclosure. This small utility area served many purposes, but it provided a good location for the first hive since it was off-limits to the public. The enclosure had two entrances: one where the West Fence Service Road terminated and a second from Rose Garden Drive near the southwestern front entrance to the gardens.

The wrought iron gate on the West Fence Service Road was locked, so Thaddeus knew the intrusion came from the Rose Garden Drive gate. Through the bars, he spotted a ghostlike figure in a white beekeeper suit with a matching hat and face screen. The hive partially blocked his view, but the noise he made unlocking the West Fence Service Road gate alerted the thief to his presence.

Space was tight in the utility enclosure, and he fast-walked the Dorsal Eighteen across to the wide-open Rose Garden Drive gate. A cut padlock and a pair of industrial-size lock cutters lay on the ground. Thaddeus looked up to catch sight of a bicycle exiting the gardens onto Botanica Drive. The rider was masked in white, and two of the hive frames were in baskets on the rear of the bike.

He fired up the Dorsal Eighteen and hopped on, helmet be damned. He rounded the corner onto the main drag and accelerated.

He was pushing the eighteen-miles-per-hour limit, but the bike ahead was on a downhill slant and still pulling away from him. When it went over a speed bump, the rider bounced, and a long gray braid fell from beneath the beekeeper's hat. Thaddeus had his suspicions before, but now he reached a ninety-nine percent certainty that Mad Maggie was the bee thief. The zeal of her Free the Bees campaign had turned into rash lawlessness and a life of crime.

Despite being sixty-some years old, Maggie was making an impressive escape. Two blocks ahead of Thaddeus, she made a sharp left turn onto Elm Street. But he knew where she was heading, and the next several blocks of her route would be uphill, slowing her down. He leaned into a tight turn as he cut left into the alley behind the Hot Rocks Café.

He fought for control of the Dorsal Eighteen on the alley cobblestones as he blasted past the café, bumping up and down and smelling a batch of Ethiopian beans cooking in the roasting drum out back. *A cup of freshly roasted coffee would be great about now*, he thought as he turned right onto Oak. He reached Elm St. and took the intersection at full throttle since the light was green, and he spotted Maggie up ahead; he had narrowed the gap to half a block. She then turned down the alley between Fir Street and Evergreen Drive. Thaddeus knew the chase was over, and the hard work would begin.

Maggie had leaned her bike against the alley-side roll-a-door of the garage at 27 Evergreen Drive. The hive frames were gone. Thaddeus heard a door slam on the yard side of the garage. He walked his Dorsal Eighteen through the gate and into the yard, where he paused to assess the situation. The garage stretched across the back end of the lot, with its far wall about two feet away from the fence separating Maggie and Cranston's property from Mable Johnson's backyard. Cranstone, sitting on the back porch, gave Thaddeus a shoulder shrug as if to say, "Nothing I can do about it." Thaddeus nodded back.

The garage's front, with its overhang jutting out four feet from the building, provided cover to the cement-slab front porch. Thaddeus wheeled his Dorsal Eighteen across the slab and leaned it against the next-to-last four-by-four support. Everything was painted eggshell white with dark green trim, reminding Thaddeus of the gazebo where the wedding took place. A porch swing hung near Thaddeus's scooter, and through the dusty front window of the garage, he noticed some movement. The only visible door was off to his left, near where he entered the yard.

"Maggie, you can't go around taking beehive frames; it's not legal," he hollered at the window. The only response was a colorful protest sign at the window that glared out Free the Bees.

Thaddeus sighed and looked back again at Cranstone, who offered another shoulder shrug before reaching over to pick up a bong on the back porch table and take a hit. He raised the bong in the air with a questioning look.

"Not now, Professor. I'm still on the job." Cranstone nodded and took another hit.

Thaddeus turned his attention back to the garage. He walked over and knocked on the garage door. "Maggie, why don't you just give me the frames, and we can talk about this later."

He heard the lock click. The door cracked open a bit, and a handful of bees flew out. He reached for the handle, and a wooden yardstick flashed out, whacking him on the back of his right hand.

"Ouch, that hurt, Maggie. Why are you smacking me with a ruler?"

He backed up from the door and noticed Cranstone grabbing the bong and heading inside. *That can't be a good sign*, he thought.

Maggie's voice drifted out from the dim interior of the garage: "I like you, Thaddeus, and you are special to Melonie, so you are special to me too. But somebody has to help the bees. A grown man like you shouldn't be picking on harmless little bees."

"But Maggie, I'm not picking on them. I'm giving them a place to live. They like it there."

"So you say, but it looks more like a prison than a home to me. Bees are free-range creatures, and they need to live in natural homes like hollowed-out trees."

Thaddeus sighed again and walked to the far end of the garage porch. He heard the door click shut and peeked around the garage's far edge to see if there was another entrance. There was not, so he leaned with his lower back against the fence bordering Mable's yard. While contemplating how to proceed, he took an unexpected smack on the back of his head. He yelped, jumped away, and turned to find Mable standing behind him with a Free the Bees sign on a three-foot pole.

He stepped back a bit to stay out of striking range and saw Adele Calhoon coming across Mable's yard carrying another protest sign and chanting, "Free the Bees." Mable appeared to have recently dyed her silver hair green, and Adele sported a mountain of hair with streaks of gray running through it at odd angles. A sinking feeling that things were rapidly spiraling out of control overwhelmed Thaddeus, and he sat on the porch swing to think.

He gently pushed with his feet to rock it back and forth and listened to the creaking coming from the eye bolts connecting the swing chain to the plywood ceiling. Feeling frustrated, he pushed his feet a bit harder, getting more lift on the swing. As the creaking increased, he noticed some bees streaming out from the left corner of the plywood ceiling. But, focused on the problem at hand, he failed to make the connection. After one last big push, he decided he would return to the botanical gardens and let things cool down. The swing moved backward, almost touching the garage, and as the action reversed into a forward motion, a new sound of cracking wood screeched out from the ceiling.

The swing's left side fell away from Thaddeus, and he pitched forward onto the lawn, where he rolled several times. From his position on the ground, he watched the front of the garage porch ceiling collapse downward while the back remained fixed against the garage. It was like a trap door from hell opening up as a fuzzy mountain of wax and honey slid down. Hundreds of pounds of it, covering his Dorsal Eighteen until only the handlebars were in sight.

From the garage, he heard a muffled voice: "Run, Thaddeus, run!"

It was only then he realized what he was seeing. The fuzziness would later be determined to consist of 30,000 bees, the largest attic hive ever found in the city.

Thaddeus got to his feet and was on the move. In his brain, he heard Jill Jammin's sequel to "Flight of the Android Bees," an equally erratic piece called "Crash of the Space Hive." He dashed toward the house as fast as he could, and to his left, he saw that Mable and Adele were almost at Mable's back door. He suddenly realized, in a moment of horror, that he was the only moving target left. *How did those old ladies outrun me?* This thought engendered a new sense of respect for the two.

On the final approach to the back-porch stairs, Thaddeus shrieked as two of the bees stabbed him in his left butt cheek. Now he sympathized with the lumbering Daniel Rump. He cleared the six steps in two strides and saw Cranstone opening the back door. Thaddeus pitched himself through the opening while Cranstone beat him over the back with the latest edition of Better Homes and Gardens, trying to squash the bees still clinging to his shirt.

By the time Thaddeus picked himself up off the floor, the bee cover on the back screen door had reduced visibility by about 70 percent. Cranston was madly hopping around, stepping on bees crawling in through a small gap in the door's left lower corner. Thaddeus grabbed a used, wet dishrag from the edge of the sink and stuffed it into the gap.

Cranstone's phone rang. Thaddeus recognized the discordant flute rifts in the ringtone as being from the second movement of "Flight of the Android Bees," the part when Rump tramples the flower beds. Cranstone answered it and listened. "Okay, you stay put for a while, darling, and don't worry. Other than a few butt stings, Thaddeus is fine." He pocketed the phone and held the bong up again.

"Yes," said Thaddeus. "I don't care if I'm still on the clock. I need medicinal treatment."

"Maggie is fine since the bees went outside and not inside the garage," said Cranstone after exhaling smoke into the air. "She also said to tell you she's sorry."

Thaddeus sat quietly at the table, pondering his next move while the cannabis did its job, bringing some measure of calm to the random neuroelectric warnings clicking around in his brain—probably adrenaline, he figured. Some of the bees were clearing off the screen door, and he stared at the six-foot hand-carved wooden totem in Maggie's garden. He recognized the artwork. It had to be from Big Luke's workshop, across the river on the northeast city limits. Thaddeus liked to occasionally wander around Luke's thirty-six-acre property and admire all the unusual carvings scattered through the woods.

Then a thought came to him unexpectedly, as insights often do. He saw a solution. A grand plan to make Maggie happy for the free-range bees, let plants benefit from nearby pollinators, and provide the gardens with a unique new piece of art. He even went so far as to imagine Jill Jammin playing a new, original composition commissioned for the unveiling entitled "The Rising Towers of Harmonious Freedom."

Anubis

Two weeks after the collapse of Maggie's attic hive, she was sitting beside Thaddeus at a large outdoor table in front of greenhouse 6 poring over a set of drawings. It was another glorious 70-degree day with clear skies. Thaddeus recalled the words of Black Elk, the Oglala Sioux shaman, describing the goodness of a perfect day: *the wind was blowing, the grass was growing, and the sky was blue.* Melonie sat on the other side of the table, smiling at the pair. She had brokered the truce between Maggie and Thaddeus with the news of Thaddeus's change of heart concerning the bees. He had even gone so far as to become a member of the Free the Bees movement.

A large sketch of the new plan for the North River Botanical Gardens' beehives was spread in front of them. As Thaddeus pointed to various parts of the plan, Maggie nodded. Thaddeus looked up and pointed toward the northeast corner of the gardens.

"From here, you'll see the tops of the totems, Maggie. Open sky and unhindered access to come and go as they please; the ultimate in freedom and all in a ninety-nine-percent natural hive. It doesn't get any better than this." Thaddeus's voice was warm and smooth, and he had his best salesman smile on.

"I like it, Thaddeus," said Maggie after a brief pause to view the sketch again. "And you promise no plastics or wire?"

"You have my word."

Maggie looked across the table at Melonie, who returned her smile. "You have impeccable taste in young men, my dear. I can see your influence in this most excellent plan."

The plan was a hundred percent Thaddeus's creation, but Melonie kept that to herself. "Just as long as you're happy, Maggie, then I'm delighted. I'm pleased as Punch."

Maggie turned to Thaddeus. "Do you know where the phrase *pleased as Punch* comes from?"

Thaddeus shook his head.

"Well, today we take it in a positive vein to indicate happiness or satisfaction. It's an idiom from the late seventeen hundreds when Punch and Judy puppet shows were popular in England. But in reality, Punch was an evil little bastard. He beat his wife and baby to death and also killed a few policemen. Every time he did someone in, he was very pleased with himself. Hence the phrase *pleased as Punch*. But I'm going to give you the benefit of the doubt that you're not knocking off our bees."

Maggie looked Thaddeus in the eye with a blue-steel gaze. He was starting to sweat, and Melonie's smile disappeared in the following moments of silence.

"Gotcha," Maggie squealed with delight as a smile returned to her face. "I know you'll do a fantastic job with this project! Give Big Luke my regards when you see him, and tell him the botanical gardens are depending on him now."

Maggie power-walked to the front gate like a small self-contained hurricane. Melonie shrugged at Thaddeus and asked when he would visit Big Luke, because she wanted to go with him. He pulled out his phone and rang Big Luke. After a bit of back and forth, they arranged a Wednesday afternoon meeting.

....

(Present)

Wednesday at noon Thaddeus meets Melonie at the Hot Rocks Café for coffee and a sandwich. After lunch, they take the Main Street Express, as the trunk-line bus route is affectionately known, and head east for a mile before the road bends to the northeast. The bus drops them off by the Arch Bridge, and they take the footpath across the river to the base of some low sandstone bluffs. From there, the walk is half a mile up a dirt road leading to Big Luke's property. A sign at the front gate informs them that they have arrived at Transformational Creations corporate headquarters.

Big Luke considers himself a transformational sculptor, turning trees into spiritual guideposts. His corporate headquarters consist of a large log cabin with a spacious front porch and a massive workshop out back. Music wafts out the front screen door. Luke is seated in a wide wooden rocking chair, keeping time with a Van Morrison piece playing low in the background. He waves them onto the porch and reaches into a cooler on his right.

"Welcome, have a seat. You have to try a pint of my latest brew. I call it *Daddy Osiris*. It's a fantastic red ale."

His dog, a medium-sized, truffle-hunting Lagotto Romagnolo, wags his tail and rolls two brown eyes upward as his only greeting. Thaddeus has met the dog several times, and he lowers the back of his hand for Anubis to sniff. He and Melonie sit in the rockers on either side of Big Luke as he pours two glasses of ale and hands them out.

Thaddeus is never one to refuse a cold beer, and he thoughtfully sips, savoring the taste. "A most excellent brew, my friend. Tell me about it. I think it has some connection to my dog friend Anubis."

Anubis wags his tail at the mention of his name, but his head remains firmly on the deck's wooden planks.

"You are correct, but let me start at the beginning for Melonie. My buddy Anubis is named after the jackal-headed Egyptian deity who watched over the embalming process and liked to escort dead kings into the afterlife. Once they arrived in the netherworld, they had to stand judgment in front of Osiris. Anubis was one of Osiris's sons. The beer is a tribute to his father." Big Luke grins from ear to ear. "When I take Anubis truffle hunting, I tell him to sniff out old Daddy Osiris."

Thaddeus chuckles, and Melonie searches for a jackal-headed creature in some of the totem poles in the front yard.

Big Luke continues: "So, Thaddeus, I gather from our conversation that you're in need of both artistic and spiritual assistance. You've come to the right place. I think I understand what you're looking for. It's important that we treat this project carefully since the botanical gardens are a critical part of the city's vital energy. But before we discuss the details, we should finish our beers and take a stroll through my gallery."

Big Luke leads the way. His gallery is spread across thirty-six acres of forest surrounding his cabin. Trails weave in and out of the trees with no apparent master plan, but about every hundred yards, the trail intersects a small, cleared circular area.

The clearings are about eighteen feet across, and each has a totem pole planted in the center. Some poles are raw wood, and others are brightly painted. But each one exhibits a stack of wild and wonderful plant and animal carvings. Some clearings have three poles, but none have just two. Thaddeus examines the totem poles and smiles. He's not sure about the numerology of Big Luke's art, but his excitement rises as he imagines the poles displayed in the botanical gardens.

"So, how tall are these?" Thaddeus asks.

Big Luke raises one of his calloused hands, motioning him to silence. "Let's bask in the spiritual vibrations of these transformations and let their wisdom guide us before we make any decisions."

Big Luke had explained before they left the porch that each pole represents the transformation of a single tree. The final totem pole contains the spiritual essence of its parent tree. The carvings allow the plants and animals of the forest to mingle with the spirit of the tree. This symbolic symbiosis acknowledges trees as the foundational species of the woodland ecosystem. There, the life and health of the entire ecosystem depend on the trees. Big Luke sees his job as transforming each tree into an artistic representation of vital energy flowing through the forest.

Rumor has it that Big Luke was a tree hugger in his early days and once spent an entire year in a makeshift tree house to keep a 300-year-old oak from being felled to make way for condos. He spent that year reading philosophy. His literary wanderings ranged from the ancient Greeks to Ludwig Wittgenstein and Bertrand Russell. After being forcibly removed from the tree, which eventually became part of the courtyard for the condos, he returned to college to double-major in art and philosophy.

Thaddeus holds his silence until they enter an area described by Big Luke as the heart of his gallery. This clearing is about twice the size of the others and positioned directly in the center is a massive totem pole, which Thaddeus guesses is forty feet tall.

"Holy crap," mutters Melonie. She also observes a jackal-headed carving about halfway up the pole.

Anubis wanders over to the pole and curls up at its base, just below the totem of a giant turtle.

Thaddeus glances around, trying to figure out how Big Luke had managed to sink three-plus tons of wood into the ground in the middle of the forest. No entry roads are apparent. It's not until they come closer that Thaddeus realizes the tree has been carved in place. He sees roots radiating out from its base.

Big Luke directs them toward three of the nine carved totem stools surrounding the central pole in a stately circle. Thaddeus sits on a beaver whose oversize front teeth protrude from the solid wood. Melonie perches on a brightly painted giant wildflower, with pinkish petals sprouting out from a dark green stem, and Big Luke takes a seat on the back of a black bear.

"Now we can talk, Thaddeus. You've seen about three-quarters of the transformations in my gallery, and I can only hope the spiritual connections have made you wiser. Whatever we do for your project must remain true to the spirits of the particular transformations we will undertake."

Thaddeus notices the wood chips tangled in Big Luke's lengthy reddish-brown beard. He imagines him as a finely carved wooden totem sitting atop a black bear. This thought sparks a marvelous idea.

Thaddeus stands, picks up a stick, and starts sketching on the ground near the mother totem pole. "I have a proposal that I want you to consider. You were quite right that we needed to observe your gallery before discussing our plans. These transformations of yours capture the essence of the forest around us. In the silence, you can feel the tendrils of Gaia's spirit gently intertwining with life and binding together this magnificent ecosystem around us. You were also right when you said that trees are a foundation species. I want to use the spirit of the tree as a foundation for life in the botanical gardens. The spirit of the forest will inhabit the gardens." By this time, Thaddeus has sketched out a totem pole with another section of a different tree trunk mounted on top of the pole. But the top section appears to be a hollowed-out log with an oval opening. Flying out from the dark interior is a bee.

Big Luke studies the drawing and scratches his beard. Anubis has risen to sniff the sketch, and pees in approval on the base of the sketched totem pole. Melonie sheds a tear because she always gets a bit emotional when Thaddeus waxes poetic about plants and ecosystems.

Big Luke gets up from his bear seat and shakes hands with Thaddeus, sealing the deal.

....
(Present)

Several months pass before the grand unveiling day. Three elegant totem poles now adorn a peaceful grassy glade tucked into the northeast quadrant of the North River Botanical Gardens. The poles create the vertices for an equilateral triangle measuring eighteen feet on each side. The base of each one is set nine feet below ground and encased in a concrete cylinder. Aboveground, the tallest of the three stretches twenty-seven feet heavenward. The tops of the other two drop down to twenty-one and fifteen feet. At Big Luke's suggestion, the tallest pole is positioned so that on the summer solstice, its sunrise shadow projects straight down Rose Garden Drive to the garden's front gate.

The crowd is starting to gather by nine in the morning, and the gardens lie beneath a crisp blue sky with a thin cover of cirrocumulus clouds creeping in from the north. Chairs and tables are arranged across the grassy carpet south of the totem poles, and near the base of the shortest pole, a podium has been installed.

Mayor Harper is slated to speak at the unveiling ceremony. Thaddeus looks around and sees him chatting with the director of the botanical gardens. He glances in the other direction and spies Maggie powering toward the mayor.

Thaddeus grabs Melonie's hand, and they intercept Maggie before she gets within shouting distance of the mayor. Mayor John Harper is Maggie's brother, and their relationship is mainly a history of bad blood. Not long ago, John had Maggie, Adele, and Mable arrested for taking her Free the Bees protest to the front doors of city hall. The charge was for holding a public protest without a permit. Maggie argued that since she and her friends were simply out for their morning stroll, the arrests amounted to illegal harassment. *People should be able to stroll in front of city hall*, she insisted. She also argued if said people chose to walk with their favorite signs, that was their business. The fact that no slogans or admonishments were being shouted disqualified their stroll from being a protest. The judge rolled his eyes before dismissing the case.

Thaddeus launches into a lengthy monologue about Big Luke's creation of the poles and the meaning of each totem carving. Maggie is too polite to walk off while Thaddeus talks, but her blue eyes keep drifting over to the mayor, and narrowing in a menacing way. As he finishes speaking about the last carving, Melonie flashes him an open hand: five minutes to go before the ceremony starts.

Thaddeus seamlessly moves on to the description of the hives. "Big Luke's real genius was the beehives on top of each totem pole," he begins, even though it was his idea. "Each one was carved from a dead tree trunk and mounted on top of its totem pole to occupy the last five feet, so no living trees were destroyed. But the part I love most is that each trunk already had a natural cavity in it. They were all destined to be homes for beehives. Luke had to enlarge them a bit, but everything about these hollowed out spaces is one hundred percent natural. The hives are up high enough so the bees and visitors won't mingle. Thanks to your efforts, Maggie, the North River Botanical Gardens will only have free-range bees."

Thaddeus successfully re-engages Maggie, and they continue their discussion until the ceremony officially starts.

Thaddeus, Melonie, and Maggie sit in the front row, and Cranstone arrives in time to sit on the other side of Maggie. Big Luke is to the right of Thaddeus, across the center aisle. Jill Jammin, who had originally been scheduled to perform the opening music, is seated beside Big Luke. They had been a couple several years back, but the tension between Jill's music and the tranquility of Luke's forest created an unresolvable rift, though they remain good friends.

Jill's signature pink-tipped hair is now raven black, as is her entire outfit: patent leather pumps, leather pants, and a tight-fitting silk blouse beneath a denim vest. Jill is in mourning; several days ago, she declared she was incapable of performing. So Harpie and Flower take the stage and open with a piece called "Falling Honey in B Major." Flower does a great job with a series of wild piccolo runs interspersed between Harpie's fast-moving bongo solos. Thaddeus notices Jill tapping her right foot and swaying with the music. Melonie had explained to Thaddeus before the ceremony that the piece was inspired by the unfortunate demise of his Dorsal Eighteen beneath the mountain of honey that fell from Maggie's garage. She laughed about it, but Thaddeus could only manage a strained smile.

Near the end of Big Luke's project, as he was working on the midheight pole, disaster struck. The hive had not yet been mounted on the pole, so its total length, including the now submerged base, was twenty-five feet. After finishing the last carving, a perched eagle surveying its domain, Big Luke started raising the pole to the vertical with a winch mechanism built on the outside of his workshop. Given the pole's two-foot diameter and its substantial length, its total weight hovered around 5,000 pounds. Big Luke always liked to view his final work raised skyward before declaring it complete.

The deities of the netherworld cast dark vibrations on Big Luke's forest that day. Unexplained, fateful events unfolded when the main cable on the winch snapped as the pole was eighty percent vertical. The pole tumbled as Anubis slept peacefully, curled up in the warm morning sun. He had been sleeping on the front porch earlier, so Big Luke assumed he was still there.

Just as the cable snapped, Big Luke cried out, "Holy shit." Loud outbursts from Big Luke were common, and Anubis's sleep was undisturbed. Through dark irony, the jackal-headed carving of the Egyptian deity Anubis, positioned twenty feet above the base, instantly killed Big Luke's faithful dog.

Even when Jill and Big Luke were living together, it was hard to know whether she was fonder of Anubis or Big Luke. Crushed by the news, she vowed she would never again play her pink Strat and immediately went into mourning.

After the music, the mayor steps up to the podium and gives a beaming politician's smile to the crowd of about fifty people. His fifteen-minute address starts with glowing praise for the director of the botanical gardens. But it becomes a bit overly effusive in describing the prominent role the gardens play in the cultural heritage of the city. Five minutes in, the mayor deftly slips into a lengthy account of the city's accomplishments under his leadership. Elections are nearing, and the mayor has reverted to stump-speech mode. In his peripheral vision, Thaddeus sees Cranstone and Melonie each gently grasp one of Maggie's arms to soothe her.

But when Mayor Harper switches to a thinly veiled attack on the Free the Bees movement, attempts to calm Maggie become visible efforts to restrain her.

Thaddeus hears Maggie say, "You dumb little fuck" through her teeth. Both Cranstone and Melonie clamp down a bit harder.

North River News has a film crew on site for a segment that will appear on their evening broadcast. Their camera pans to Maggie, who, with a politician's instinct, flashes a benign, slightly sad smile that can only be interpreted as "Poor Mayor John."

The mayor finishes his speech with an announcement clearly aimed at the news crew in the hopes that he will get some free publicity. "Our city is perched on the edge of an exciting future. The botanical gardens are a fine example of how we are gaining international fame. I'm sure the awards received last year are only a glimpse of what's to come. With the theme of progress in mind, I am also pleased to announce that negotiations are starting for a stunning new condominium development along the north bank of the river directly across from these beautiful gardens. Progress is coming, my friends. Thank you for celebrating with us this morning."

Cranstone is leaning heavily to his right to keep Maggie in her seat, and Melonie's back is straight with her shoulder muscles tensed. She has been leading the ecological rehabilitation team responsible for restoring the north bank into a swath of open parkland and natural riparian habitats. Thaddeus knows the mayor has just punched a hole in her plans. The proposed development by Condo Carl, which she believed was off the table, is now firmly back in play.

The mayor has left the podium and is exiting the ceremony via the grassy central aisle dividing the audience when Melonie makes her decision. She releases Maggie's arm. Cranstone almost falls from his seat as Maggie bolts up and screams: "You've gone too far now, you little half-wit. You're going down."

In a prescient bit of musical genius, Harpie starts in with a galloping beat on the bongos. Flower exchanges her piccolo for a flute and leans into the microphone to lay down the "William Tell Overture" on top of Harpie's beat. She skips the very beginning and starts in with the rolling melody of the second segment. Thaddeus is already on the move, but he pauses momentarily to marvel at how Harpie's beat matches Maggie's footsteps. Thaddeus is particularly fond of this piece and can't get it out of his head as the action unfolds before him.

The mayor looks over his shoulder in time to see Maggie rounding the corner seats onto the central aisle. He starts to run, but Maggie is already at full speed and lunges for him just as he passes the last row of chairs. She firmly snags his belt, pulling his pants down to his knees. He stumbles forward and sprawls out facedown on the freshly mowed grass. Maggie is on him like a pro wrestler, putting him in a vicious headlock with her left arm and using her right-hand knuckles to give him a vigorous noogie.

"Stop it, Maggie," he hollers. "That hurts. I just had a hair transplant up there."

Thaddeus notices the mayor's emerald-green boxers covered in Dr. Seuss characters. The Grinch is positioned over the mayor's right butt cheek. He starts to thrash in an attempt to free himself, but Maggie clings to his back and wraps her legs around her little brother's waist, evoking the image she is riding a wild bull. But nothing interferes with the rapid noogie action on his sore skull.

Thaddeus glances at the film crew as he and Cranstone run down the center aisle. He can tell from their smiles that they can't believe their lucky stars. The rest of the audience is stunned and motionless.

Thaddeus, Cranstone, and two men from the back row try to lift Maggie off the mayor but to no avail. She is virtually welded onto his back at this point.

The "William Tell Overture" has stopped. Harpie now produces a rising drum roll like you might expect at the circus before the human cannonball is fired. The men succeed in raising the pair a foot off the ground and shake them until Mayor Harper breaks loose and is unceremoniously dumped to the ground. Flower lets out an ear-splitting screech on the flute as his body drops. The mayor scrambles away and stands while pulling his pants up.

"You've lost your mind, Maggie Harper. This is the last straw. I'm pressing assault charges."

Cranstone has a tight grip on Maggie, but she has relaxed and flashes a friendly smile as the camera pans in her direction. "Sorry, little brother. Are you having a bad day?"

Mayor Harper, with his back to the camera, exits as fast as he can while still maintaining a dignified gait. Thaddeus reflects that this is the third time Maggie has publicly pantsed the mayor, and threats of assault charges never materialized from the first two spectacles.

Thaddeus and Melonie order in that evening and enjoy a few slices of pizza with cold IPAs as the six o'clock news comes on. Connie Carter, the show's anchor, starts with "Mayor Harper pantsed again by his big sister." The film crew did an admirable job of capturing the action. They even got a close-up of the Grinch. Thaddeus enjoys hearing Harpie and Flower's rendition of the overture again. In the background, he sees Jill, standing like a shadow, possibly contemplating a musical ballad of the day's events. Her right foot is tapping to Harpie's beat. No mentions of the mayor's accomplishments or the north bank deal make the final cut.

The Flaming Dogs of Lake Huron

Three days after the unveiling ceremony at the botanical gardens, Big Luke's send-off for Anubis took place at Shorty's Waterfront Bar.

The river curved at the Arch Bridge and diverted from its southeast-to-northwest trend through the city to a more north–south path. Upriver from the bridge lay Devil Woods Dam. The dam was constructed in the late 1800s at a natural waterfall to provide waterpower for mills and factories, and it played a prominent role in the early development of the city. The dam went through several modifications over the next five decades, but the last of these occurred during the Great Depression. However, another fifty years passed before the city cleaned up the area and built a large waterfront park with easy access for recreational activities on the lake-like section above the dam, where the water stayed deep and calm.

Shorty's Waterfront Bar was a quarter of a mile south of the dam on the river's east bank. His family had owned land from above the sandstone bluffs to the waterfront for as long as anyone could remember. Rick, Shorty's dad, built the original bar, a ramshackle wooden dive called Rick's Place. It was better known for its late-night barroom fights than its menu, but it paid the bills and kept Shorty's family warm, dry, and fed.

Shorty worked the bar with his dad until Rick died in an unfortunate incident involving a derelict water tower. Shorty was then free to pursue his vision, and he secured a loan to upgrade to Shorty's Waterfront Bar. Shorty didn't have a business degree, but he was a shrewd businessman. His establishment had become the premier location for passing lazy summer afternoons and pleasant evenings by the water. His fabulous chef, Georgie, kept the customers coming back.

One of Shorty's latest additions to the thriving business was a massive floating dock jutting out from the riverbank, where customers could dine or rent it out for private functions. This outdoor space effectively doubled his seating capacity for those busy weekends during his peak summer season.

Big Luke had booked the floating platform for this evening's memorial for Anubis. When he originally booked the event, Shorty imagined that the description of the event as a send-off was a figurative reference to saying goodbye. Big Luke and Shorty were more acquaintances than friends, but he had met Anubis on several occasions and knew Big Luke loved the dog.

The afternoon before the memorial, Shorty had seen Big Luke kayaking about thirty yards off the shore in front of the floating platform, presumably getting the lay of the land. He didn't notice Big Luke drop a forty-pound concrete block into the water. He also didn't see the retractable cable, with one end attached to an eye hook in the concrete and the other end holding on to the edge of the platform.

....

(Present)

Thaddeus and Melonie arrive at Shorty's Waterfront Bar by Uber and spy Maggie and Cranstone getting out of their car. The four stroll across the parking lot toward the floating platform. A dozen or so people have already arrived, and most of them are standing on the riverside edge of the platform, admiring a western sky on fire with crimson and pink as the sun drops toward the horizon. Thaddeus can make out Jill and Big Luke carrying a long bundle from his truck and placing it on the far edge of the platform. He considers Big Luke's life equation, where relationships carry a heavy weighting, but keeps his thoughts to himself since Melonie, Maggie, and Cranstone are entranced watching the sunset.

As they approach the platform, Melonie points out the six-foot-tall Marshall amp sitting on its right, riverside edge. Thaddeus then sees a jet-black Strat in a guitar stand by the amp. Halfway down the platform, in a shoreward direction, is Jill's pink Strat. Thaddeus thinks it will be an interesting evening.

Big Luke has gone all out for his guests, with several tables of Georgie's best hors d'oeuvres and an ample supply of Daddy Osiris red ale. By the time the sun disappears and twilight creeps across the calm river water, about three dozen people have arrived.

Big Luke starts the ceremony with a moment of silence and then launches into tender but humorous stories about Anubis. He ends with a toast to the exotic and mysterious nature of life, counseling his guests to live each day fully, as Anubis did. Large cups of red ale are raised with the chant "Godspeed, Anubis."

"Now let's be silent as we send Anubis on his way," announces Big Luke. "Afterward, Jill will play a tribute called 'Ode to Anubis in F-sharp

Minor."'

Several people glance around in mild confusion. Melonie breathes a soft "Oh no" that only Thaddeus can hear.

Jill and Big Luke solemnly walk to the bundle on the edge of the dock, remove the tarp cover, and lower it into the water. Big Luke lights a torch and hands it to Jill, who throws it on top of the dark floating shape. The retracting cable immediately starts pulling the funeral pyre toward the center of the river. Flames illuminate Anubis atop cedar bows, dried kindling, and a layer of small logs.

Before the crowd fully absorbs what they are seeing, Jill picks up the black Strat, loops it over her left shoulder, and lays into a wild version of "The Star-Spangled Banner." Her music is eerily reminiscent of Jimi Hendrix's Woodstock performance. The hair on the back of Thaddeus's neck seems to vibrate and swirl with the acoustic energy blasting out of the giant Marshall amp. It whips across the platform like wind from an apocalyptic storm.

Big Luke walks over to Thaddeus and Melonie. He is smiling and swaying to the music, clearly pleased with how the evening is progressing. Thaddeus looks toward the restaurant and sees that all of Shorty's customers have stopped eating, and most are gathered by the deck railing with drinks in their hands, watching the show. Several have even placed a hand over their heart. One man stands at attention, giving a full salute.

Jill finishes, leans into the microphone, and says, "Now, an ode to my dear friend Anubis." As she turns the Strat volume down a notch, she glances over her right shoulder at the funeral pyre, which has now reached the halfway point in its journey.

Flames leap six feet in the air as the burn accelerates, and some signs of nervous tension appear throughout the crowd. Big Luke didn't share the details of the evening with anyone except Jill, and most guests arrived believing they were attending a quaint tribute and memorial service.

Thaddeus reflects on how life sometimes creeps up and springs out from its shadowy hiding places. He realizes Maggie might be the only guest to completely roll with it and get into the groove of the evening. She had sung her way through the entire "Star Spangled Banner."

Melonie relaxes a bit as Jill uses her loop pedal to record sixteen bars of rhythm using several variations of F-sharp minor, B minor, C-sharp minor, and A major chords. The loop starts playing, and Jill delicately dances her left hand up and down the fretboard, producing a hauntingly soulful melody. As the piece progresses, she keeps an eye on Anubis. The funeral boat is riding lower in the water and nearing its destination when Jill starts yapping and howling into the microphone. The effect could have been overly chaotic, but Jill pulls it off with no trouble. Somewhere echoing in the background, Thaddeus swears he hears Janice Joplin.

Big Luke leans in close and whispers to Thaddeus, "This is the part where the flaming dogs of Lake Huron beckon Anubis into the netherworld."

Thaddeus is thankful that Melonie had once explained the original composition to him. Several years ago, Jill wrote and performed a locally famous piece called "The Flaming Dogs of Lake Huron." It tracks the tale of an intelligent species of dogs imprisoned by alien cats on an island in the northern reaches of Lake Huron. They try to escape by constructing hydrogen zeppelins to drift with the wind to the mainland. But the mandate of heaven was not with them on the fateful day of their escape. Bolts of lightning from a rogue thunderstorm ignite their zeppelins, turning them into fireballs, and they drop from the sky into the waters of Lake Huron. The dogs descend to the bottom of the lake, and their souls travel to meet Osiris, who grants them sanctuary in the netherworld.

Thaddeus appreciates the music even more since he understands the background. In his mind's eye, Anubis trots down a dimly illuminated path toward the howling calls of his predecessors.

Jill's music slowly fades as Anubis's boat finally reaches its resting place directly above the concrete block Luke had placed on the river bottom. The flames are starting to smolder, and the boat is riding low in the water. Jill puts down the black Strat and retrieves the pink one while Big Luke motions the crowd back from the center of the platform. Jill pauses, and the pyre light flickers off the tears on her cheeks. She grips the neck of the guitar and hollers in a choked voice, "This is for you, Anubis."

With that declaration, she starts spinning like an Olympic discus thrower. She takes three twirls, each one bringing her closer to the edge of the dock. With one final heave, the pink Strat goes airborne in a long arc toward the sinking remains of the funeral pyre as it disappears below the surface. The Strat travels halfway to the smoldering pyre before reaching the water and sliding without a splash into the dark. Big Luke has slipped away toward the Marshall amp.

The crowd becomes visibly distressed when they see more chaos is yet to come—several shriek "no" as Jill charges the amp and hits it with a full body slam. The amp shifts closer to the water, and its back wheels slip off the platform. Jill bounces several feet back toward the center of the platform. Big Luke pulls her in close with his left arm as she starts to charge the amp a second time, holding her off the ground and rubbing her shoulders with his right hand while she sobs.

Crowd nervousness rises, and there is a rapid shift to the other end of the platform opposite the amp. This movement causes the whole structure to rock, and the teetering amp slips into the river with a sizzling pop. Shorty's Waterfront bar goes dark as the main breaker flips.

No one is sure what to do next, and a stunned, pungent silence hangs over the guests. But in the darkness of the restaurant behind them, the sounds of clapping and dog whistles start to fill the air as Shorty's customers express their approval. The platform crowd regains its mental balance, and a slow chant grows: "Anubis, Anubis, Anubis…" Moonlight provides enough visibility for the memorial guests to find the beer table, and another round of Daddy Osiris is dispensed.

Thaddeus stands looking over the calm black waters of the river, sipping a cup of ale. No signs of the floating funeral pyre or the pink Strat remain. The evening had proven to be quite an unexpected adventure. He turns back to the shoreline and realizes there is more to come when flashing red and blue lights veer off the main highway and head down the road to Shorty's Waterfront Bar. About the time the police car parks, the lights come back on, and Thaddeus watches people on the deck refill their drinks. He recognizes Officer Trudeau, who engages Shorty in conversation. The parking lot lights give a black-and-white feel to the scene, like a soundless movie track. Shorty's animated movements add to the effect as he waves his arms in the air, shrugs his shoulders, and points toward the middle of the river in the direction of the sunken funeral pyre. Officer Trudeau turns to observe the guests on the floating platform, and they raise their cups of red ale in the air, shouting, "Anubis." The officer proceeds to the restaurant and interviews a few customers.

After interviewing Shorty's customers on the restaurant deck, Officer Trudeau takes a leisurely stroll across the parking lot to walk onboard the floating platform. Shorty follows him.

Jack shakes Big Luke's hand and offers his condolences. "Is it true you buried him at sea on a funeral pyre?"

Big Luke is relaxed and seems a hundred percent okay with the situation. "Yeah, Jack. You know, he was a great dog, and he needed a proper goodbye."

"Sorry, Big Luke," Shorty jumps in. "I didn't mind, but some of the neighbors on the bluff saw the fire and called 9-1-1. They thought it was my dock."

"Don't worry about it, Shorty." Big Luke turns back to Jack. "Shorty had no idea about the funeral pyre. I sort of arranged things on the sly this afternoon."

Jack rubs his chin. "So, Big Luke, I'm sure you know that burning a boat on the water within city limits is against the law. I don't recall any ordinances specifically mentioning burning a boat with a corpse on it, but I'm sure that's also illegal."

Big Luke nods. "You got me there."

Jack sees Thaddeus and gives him a wave. They had worked together on the bee theft case.

"Shorty, are you pressing charges?"

"No way, officer."

Jack's attention returns to Big Luke. "Okay, I'm going to have to issue you a citation and a one-thousand-dollar fine. You have the right to contest it if you want to, but—"

Big Luke interrupts by holding his hand up, palm out. "I will be down at city hall first thing in the morning to pay the fine."

Jack nods, indicating they are done, and turns to face Jill, who is standing about nine feet to his left. He motions with his finger. "Ms. Jammin, we need to have a word. By the way, I am a big fan. The customers on the deck told me I missed quite a show."

Jill smiles. "Thank you, officer. I presume this is about the amp and my pink guitar."

"Yes, ma'am. Are you going to replace the pink Stratocaster?"

"No, I swore I'd never play the pink Strat again when I heard of Anubis's untimely demise." She starts to choke up again with a few tears. "Maybe a lime green or neon blue, though."

Jack pauses so she can regain her composure. "I'm sorry, Ms. Jammin, but I'll have to give you a citation plus a two-hundred-and-fifty dollar fine for littering in a public waterway."

"I'll pay that one also tomorrow morning," says Big Luke.

The officer looks around. "I think that wraps things up here unless you have anything else for me, Shorty."

Shorty shakes his head no.

"Okay, folks. Enjoy the rest of your evening, and take a cab home if you've been sipping too much of Big Luke's ale."

Thaddeus watches Officer Trudeau's car vanish down the main highway and wonders about the man's life equation.

Harper versus Harper

Elections were nearing for North River, and several issues roiled below the surface of the city's usually benign politics. Mayor Harper's recent announcement of a possible north bank development agitated the ecologically minded, and Proposition 420 created ample cultural tension between marijuana enthusiasts and the less liberally minded.

Thaddeus disliked politics and had avoided the subject whenever possible for his entire life thus far. It's not that he didn't think about politics, nor was he an un-civic-minded lout who couldn't be bothered to vote. Thaddeus had made a point of voting in every election since he turned eighteen. He also researched every candidate and proposition and always filled out the entire ballot—informed voting on every competitive issue was a matter of personal responsibility and a cornerstone of democracy. Thaddeus just didn't enjoy talking about politics.

His reticence to join in the mindless discourse stemmed from his observation that most political discussions appeared to have no basis in fact or critical thinking. The banal wittering that passed for public debate seemed an appalling waste of time. When Cranstone explained his delusional humanism theory, Thaddeus finally found a philosophical basis for his aversion to discussing politics.

But politics was now getting personal for Thaddeus. His patents on Gaia Gold and his consulting contracts with Grant's New Amsterdam greenhouse business had proven lucrative. He was making considerably more money each month from these ventures than from his paycheck at the North River Botanical Gardens. Demand for Gaia Gold was booming; it was the most sought-after crop on the legal cannabis market. Grant had opened a second greenhouse strictly dedicated to growing Gaia Gold. After his income from royalties and consulting fees reached $270,000, Melonie advised him to invest in equities and bonds since the interest paid out on his savings account didn't even cover the cost of inflation.

Thaddeus took Melonie's advice and read a book on investing. The only thing he learned was that he would rather spend his time working in the gardens than researching investments. Still, Melonie was right.

So, after a bit more research, Thaddeus located Joseph Pool, a financial manager with ties to a national firm where fiduciary duties were serious business. He wasn't going down the Bernie Madoff rat hole.

Joseph recommended a long-term outlook for financial growth, investing money he wouldn't need for at least a decade in equities and keeping some shorter-term investments in bonds and CDs. Thaddeus followed Joseph's advice and periodically transferred money to his accounts when his bank balance got too fat. Thaddeus was a simple guy with simple needs, and his paycheck from the botanical gardens was sufficient.

The political dilemma he found himself in stemmed from Proposition 420. Lifestyle conflicts were at work in North River. After the legalization of marijuana, a number of residents had reduced their intake of alcohol; a light buzz at happy hour was more than enough. Consequentially, alcohol consumption was trending downward. This shift in evening relaxation habits was bad news for Larry Oligard. Larry's Liquor was the largest retailer of spirits in North River, with stores throughout the city.

Grant had recently stirred up a hornet's nest when he started an advertising campaign with the slogan "Liquor Kills You Quicker—Grow Old With Gaia Gold." This was the last straw for Larry, and he collected enough signatures to get Proposition 420 on the ballot. It sought to make cannabis shops illegal in North River.

Thaddeus had to be honest with himself on the political front. While he was professionally interested in growing the best marijuana in the world, he also enjoyed his financial security. Sure that Melonie was the one, he saw them possibly buying a house in the not-too-distant future. He hadn't actually asked her the big question, but he sensed that moment coming closer.

Politics was also creeping into other aspects of his life as indignation swelled over the north bank commercial development project. After the mayor's announcement at the unveiling ceremony, Melonie did some digging. She was at the eye of this storm since she was the team lead for the city's North Bank Ecological Rehabilitation Project.

As she suspected, the ongoing negotiations the mayor referenced were with Carl Blankers, aka Condo Carl, one of the city's largest real estate developers. He had a habit of cutting inside deals with local governments, so taxpayers funded expensive improvements to a development project before he started building. This tactic cut down on his total financial investment and increased his profits. There was no question that luxury condos on the riverfront would carry hefty price tags and generate big profits.

Melonie was not surprised when a bond initiative appeared on the ballot. The bonds would fund a massive investment in a riverfront amphitheater and extensive boardwalks along most of the riverfront. This was just the type of activity Melonie's team was trying to stop. Riparian ecosystems on the riverbanks would become nonexistent, and the rainwater runoff from walkways and large parking areas associated with the project would be a pollution threat. Melonie understood that if she could kill the bond initiative, Condo Carl would abandon plans to develop the area. Unlike Thaddeus, Melonie had no aversion to entering the political fray.

Both Larry and Condo Carl were large contributors to Mayor John Harper's campaign. Thaddeus pondered his dilemma as he worked on a new clematis garden under construction in the southeast quadrant of the botanical gardens. He knew his hand would soon be forced, and undoubtedly the ensuing changes would unbalance his life equation. He stoically accepted the facts because he knew there was no retreat into the past. Life only moved in one direction, and that was forward into the future.

....

(Present)

Thaddeus leaves work early and takes a leisurely stroll toward Melonie's condo. She called him earlier in the day excited about a new project she wanted to discuss, and he promised her he would be there by four. He has a full half hour, so he dallies at the Hot Rocks Café, ordering a cup of green tea and admiring the latest artwork. The exhibition is a one-man show by Søren, a local artist. Thaddeus recognizes the name; the North River Fine Arts Museum purchased one of his creations last year. That piece won acclaim at a national art festival, and since Søren was homegrown North River talent, acquiring it was a no-brainer.

Søren is deeply into his negative-space phase, and the five paintings on the walls of the Hot Rocks Café garner Thaddeus's attention. The compositions reflect a fusion art style, merging photography and acrylics. The photos were processed with digital modifications and printed on four-foot-by-four-foot canvases. Søren then partially painted over the digital artwork. The images are all done in a gray-scale palette. Thaddeus recently read an interview with the artist and recalled his description. "My work lets form and composition emerge from nothingness, and the negative space allows the viewer's imagination to derive a unique interpretation of the art."

Thaddeus is taken with a painting showing a dirt road leading to a farmhouse. A photo has been digitally modified by abstracting the composition and letting it fade into grays and whites on the right side of the canvas. As the digital work fades, Søren's acrylic painting picks up with delicate washes over the original image. The upper right of the final image is comprised of negative space filled with faint swirling gray undulations like a mist or fog blocking the view. Thaddeus is captivated even though the price tag is $5,000.

He finishes his tea and goes to find Carol, the café owner. "Could you tell the artist I'd like to buy the piece with the road and farmhouse?" He points to the painting on the north wall.

"Sure, Thaddeus. Søren will be thrilled to have another local patron. Is it for Melonie?"

"Maybe," he replies with a smile. "I don't think she's ever seen it, and we all know that art is in the eye of the beholder. We'll see."

Thaddeus gives Carol his phone number and checks his watch: ten minutes left.

He arrives at Melonie's at exactly four o'clock and lets himself in. Melonie, Maggie, and Grant are huddled around the kitchen table. He shoots Melonie a questioning look.

Melonie flashes that smile he loves. "Thaddeus, we're having a campaign meeting."

Thaddeus feels the winds of change blowing harder. "And, what are we campaigning for?"

Maggie looks up with her blue eyes burning bright. The same look she had when she protested to free the bees. "I'm going to be North River's next mayor. Melonie's managing my campaign, and Grant is the treasurer. We're brainstorming our fundraising strategy. That half-wit brother of mine already has fifty thousand dollars in his war chest. I'd be honored if you would help us out."

Grant has a mild expression of resignation, and Thaddeus assumes Maggie and Grant have reached a truce over the beehives, which are still on the roof to the best of his knowledge. *Maggie Harper versus John Harper will be an epic campaign contest,* was all Thaddeus could think. He has a hefty bank balance waiting for transfer to his investment accounts with Joseph, but he realizes the political landscape requires his attention.

"I'm looking at your key campaign staff, Maggie, and I assume you're running against Proposition 420 and the north bank bond initiative."

"Affirmative on both counts, Thaddeus."

"Do you have a campaign bank account?" Thaddeus directs his question to Grant, who nods. "Who do I make the check out to?"

Maggie pipes up again: "Maggie for Mayor."

Thaddeus retrieves his checkbook from the study and writes a check while standing at the kitchen counter. Between the artwork and the campaign contribution, he empties his bank account but is unbothered; beyond food and shelter, money is a minor term in Thaddeus's life equation. But he understands that money lubricates the wheels of politics and considers the campaign contribution as money well spent. He ponders whether Maggie will pants Mayor John again during the campaign.

Grant raises his eyebrows after Thaddeus hands him the check. "Well, Maggie, you are now evenly funded with your brother."

Melonie gives him a *Holy Crap!* look followed by an approving smile, and Thaddeus shrugs.

Maggie puts on her best smile and says, "Thanks. I knew I could count on a fine young man like you."

Grant lights a joint and passes it around the table.

Cranstone shows up at Melonie's at 5:50 p.m., and they all watch the six o'clock news. The music plays, and slick graphics slide smoothly across the screen before Connie Carter's face takes center stage on the seventy-inch television.

"This is Connie Carter bringing you the latest news from North River. The mayor's race heated up this morning when Maggie Harper, the mayor's older sister, officially announced her candidacy. You heard right: it's Harper versus Harper this year." In the background, the footage of Maggie pantsing her brother at the unveiling ceremony replays and freezes on a close-up of his Dr. Seuss boxers. "The question on everyone's mind is, will the mayor get pantsed again by his older sister? Let's hear what Maggie Harper had to say this morning."

Footage of Maggie's morning interview with Erika Cool appears on the screen, replacing Connie. "This is Erika Cool with North River News. I'm here with Maggie Harper. Maggie, why are you challenging your brother for mayor?"

"Erika, you look lovely today, my dear. You know, I have a long history of working for social justice in North River. For too long, I've watched while my little brother made a mess of our city. But I'm afraid he's gone too far this time with Proposition 420 and the North Bank Development Bond Issue. Between you and me, he has always had an authoritarian streak. I'm here to say that as mayor, I will fight for the North Bank Ecological Rehabilitation Project, and I oppose the government's efforts to drive honest businesses out of town with Proposition 420. Johnny stands for the interests of big real estate and liquor stores. I'm more interested in serving the needs of city residents, not big business."

"Maggie, will you be pantsing the mayor again?"

"Oh, that was just a small family disagreement, dear. Of course, on the campaign trail, I will respect Johnny's views. I'm here to improve the quality of life in North River and run a positive campaign fighting for the rights and freedoms of North River's residents."

Thaddeus is impressed at Maggie's on-camera presence. He also knows that her little brother hates to be called Johnny.

The camera cuts back to Connie. "And now let's take you live to city hall, where Erika Cool is interviewing our mayor."

Erika is standing on the sidewalk, almost in the same location where she interviewed Maggie that morning. She intercepted Mayor John as he was leaving his office. "Mr. Mayor, what's your reaction to your sister's challenge?"

"Thank you, Erika. I think we all understand that my sister is not a serious candidate. She is just pulling another one of her publicity stunts."

"Candidate Maggie Harper says you are ignoring the needs of the people with your support for the North Bank Bond initiative and Proposition 420. Can you comment on that?"

"The north bank development will bring jobs and much-needed housing to the city. This development will benefit everyone."

"Mayor, we have obtained information indicating the condos planned by Carl Blankers will sell for over a million dollars apiece. How does this benefit the people of North River, who will be taxed to subsidize this luxury development?"

Maggie leaps up off the couch. "Stick it to the little twerp, Erika." She pumps her fist in the air several times.

Melonie taps her on the arm. "Remember what we discussed about name-calling."

Maggie sits down, but there is still a big smile on her face.

Mayor John fumbles over the answer. "Well, Erika, people living in these condos will need services like house cleaning and landscaping." He realizes how bad this sounds and tries to smooth things over. "And, after, all the people in those condos will pay higher property taxes."

Erika lets that hang before asking her last question. "Public records show that Carl Blankers and Larry Oligard are your two biggest campaign contributors. Mr. Blankers clearly has a vested interest in the north bank development, and Mr. Oligard is the owner of Larry's Liquor and the organizer of Proposition 420. Do you care to comment?"

The pitch of the mayor's voice rises as he becomes mildly agitated. "There are no improprieties here. The bond initiative and Proposition

420 are for the public to approve or not approve as they see fit."

A campaign aide appears on camera and whispers in the mayor's ear. "I'm sorry, Erika, but there's been a slight emergency, and I need to go back to my office."

"Emergency, my ass," says Maggie.

"This is Erika Cool at city hall. Back to you, Connie."

The team agrees that, on the whole, news coverage on the first day of the campaign was quite positive.

The next morning Thaddeus arrives at work and returns to the new clematis garden to find half of the plants hanging loosely on their poles with roots pulled out of the ground. He takes his time replanting the roots but still has to remove six plants for emergency care in greenhouse 9. After careful inspection, he determines that humans, not animals, were the cause.

Thaddeus is having a light lunch at his desk when his phone rings with an unknown caller. The number is local, so he answers.

"Mr. Barcelona, this is Søren. Carol told me you are interested in one of my works on display at the Hot Rocks Café. I'm delighted."

"Søren, thanks for getting in touch, and please, call me Thaddeus."

"Well, Thaddeus, I have to say that I love what you've done with the botanical gardens over the past several years. And between you and me, I'm also a Gaia Gold fan. You probably didn't realize I was in the audience at the dedication of Big Luke's totem pole project a week or so ago."

"No, I didn't realize you were at the unveiling."

"The whole event was quite entertaining, in my opinion. I was one of the men who helped you and Maggie's husband shake her loose from her poor brother. I don't know whether I enjoyed the live event or the evening news coverage more." Søren chuckles softly.

"At any rate, Søren, I was quite taken with *Road to Buddha's Farm*. I'm hoping to purchase it if it's still up for sale."

"It most certainly is. I can meet you at the café tomorrow afternoon at four if you're available."

"It's already on my calendar." Another idea springs from the shadows and enters Thaddeus's mind. "Did you know that Maggie declared her candidacy for mayor yesterday?"

"I didn't. I was locked away in my studio until midnight."

"My girlfriend, Melonie, is her campaign manager. Would you be interested in helping with the art and social media aspects of the campaign?"

"It's funny you should ask, Thaddeus. I have been thinking about getting more involved in social media videos. Yes, as long as she is against Proposition 420, I'm interested."

"Is it okay if I give Melonie your phone number?"

"Of course. I'll see you tomorrow at Hot Rocks."

Proposition 420

The first week of Maggie's campaign was full of bustle and excitement as the team coalesced. Melonie engaged with Søren, who readily agreed to be the campaign's artistic director. Grant and Melonie continued fundraising and, by the end of the week, had secured another $9,000 in small contributions. Maggie used her Free the Bees connections to form a small army of canvassers who went door-to-door each day to convince voters that Maggie was the future of North River.

Mayor John had served three terms in office, and the lack of credible competition had left him with a weak canvassing team, who primarily relied on his incumbent status in their sales pitches. Maggie was determined to take advantage of this. To her surprise, pantsing her brother at the unveiling ceremony had generated a lot of positive name recognition. The average voter was coolly neutral on the current mayor, often unable to recount anything he had done over the last term other than collect a nice paycheck.

Maggie's campaign strategy firmed up during that first week, and she announced that as mayor, she would donate her mayoral paychecks to volunteer food pantries and other local charities for her full term in office. "No Hungry Children" became one of her campaign slogans. She and Melonie also agreed to focus on Proposition 420 for the first several weeks and then transition to the North Bank Development Bond. Connie Carter's morning show influenced that strategy by contacting Maggie and the mayor for a live appearance on Tuesday to discuss Proposition 420.

John Harper's strong points did not include ad-libbing in public, but Maggie had turned public spectacles into a fine art form. She was comfortably in her groove when winging it during a live conversation.

Søren was on a roll as well, embracing his new role with gusto. He secured city permits for filming their first campaign ad, also on Tuesday, on Main Street and hoped to have a final cut ready by Friday. He was quite excited and offered to support the campaign by funding the cost of video shoots.

Maggie arrives at the North River News production studio an hour before the morning show starts. She dresses for the occasion in jeans and a long-sleeve turquoise top beneath a black silk vest. Her signature red high-top Converse sneakers finish off the outfit. The mayor has not arrived, so Maggie walks around the set with Connie to get a feel for the layout. She checks out her seat and considers the lighting before tying an emerald-green bow at the bottom of her silvery gray braid and then draping it over her right shoulder. She asks the camera operator to zoom in while she checks out the visual effect on a side monitor. She flips the braid over the other shoulder and examines the look from another angle.

"Maggie, that green is suspiciously close to the color of your brother's underwear," says Connie with a frown. "He only consented to do this show when you agreed not to bring up the pantsing."

"Don't worry, dear. I won't mention it. But I've been surprised by the number of voters I speak to who loved your coverage of the unveiling ceremony."

Connie smiles but withholds any comment. She loses focus for a moment as she concentrates on her earpiece. "The mayor has just arrived." After glancing at her wristwatch, she adds, "You may want to go to makeup and let them dress you up a bit for the camera."

Maggie sees John as she enters her dressing room and waves. He eyes her and doesn't reciprocate.

The stage is set with a center chair for Connie, Maggie to her right, and Mayor John to her left. A low table with carefully arranged magazines sits in front of the threesome, giving the effect of a morning chat over a cup of coffee. Connie listens to her earpiece as the producer says to her, "One minute to cameras."

Maggie notices that John is wearing suspenders, a new look for him. When he shifts his suit jacket, she sees that the suspenders are sewn into his pants. He seems unconscious of the fact that viewers will also see this when the camera zooms in.

The floor manager holds up his fingers for five, four, three, two, one, and points to Connie as the cameras roll.

"Welcome to The Morning Show, folks. I'm Connie Carter, and I have our two mayoral candidates with me today. Mayor John Harper"—she motions to her left—"and his sister, Maggie Harper. Thank you both for being here this morning to discuss Proposition 420. For our viewers, if you aren't familiar with this ballot proposition, it seeks to outlaw cannabis shops here in North River. Mr. Mayor, why don't you tell us why you support this proposition."

"Thank you for having me today, Connie. It's a pleasure to be here. We all know that cannabis was legalized in our state several years ago, but local governments were given the authority to determine if cannabis retail stores could operate within the city limits. We initially allowed these shops on a trial basis, but it has become quite apparent that they attract a certain undesirable clientele and even some criminal elements. I support Proposition 420 from a public safety standpoint."

Connie followed up with, "A recent poll showed nearly fifty percent of participants occasionally used cannabis. Don't they deserve to shop for it without having to travel?"

"Connie, I support a person's right to use cannabis. I just believe these shops are frequented by people who can pose a threat to our community. I think most voters would agree."

The camera pulls out wide, and Maggie reaches into her inner vest pocket. She produces a beautifully rolled joint of Gaia Gold and tosses it onto the coffee table. The mayor, who was about to say something, stops with his mouth hanging open, and even Connie looks surprised. The camera zooms in on the creamy white stick of ganja, slowly rolling across the tabletop. After it stops, the shot frames Maggie and Connie, cutting the mayor out of view.

"Is this what you're afraid of, Johnny? Is this small little stick of paper and weed really the public safety hazard you refer to? Last year ninety-five percent of DUIs in our city were attributed to alcohol. Over the past four years since cannabis was legalized, the city has reported two hundred and seventy deaths from alcohol and zero from cannabis. I take the occasional toke, and I also like a cold beer or a glass of wine. But go to a liquor store, and you find spirits with up to ninety percent alcohol. That shit is lethal. It'll make you go blind. And here you are, picking on enterprising small-business owners of cannabis stores and letting our liquor store owners off the hook. You have your priorities wrong, Mr. Mayor, and that's why I'm gonna take you down."

The slight delay lets the producer bleep out the word *shit* before the viewers hear it. But Maggie is sure they will get the message.

Connie is clearly pleased with the action flaming up on her morning show. "So Maggie. Would you outlaw liquor stores?"

"Certainly not. This is a free country, and I have faith in voters' judgment. The fact that cannabis sales are up and liquor sales are down is no reason for our city to interfere with the free market and take sides. It's possible that Mayor John and his buddies, like the owner of Larry's

Liquor, Mr. Oligard, might just want to control who profits. By the way, Larry Oligard is the driving force behind getting Proposition 420 on the ballot in the first place. That should tell us something."

The discussion continues on a downward spiral for the mayor. He checks his watch several times, wondering when the pain will end.

As the show winds up, Maggie flips her braid over the front of her left shoulder so the emerald-green bow pops out against her black vest and offers a parting comment. "By the way, brother, I like the look of your new suspenders. Those babies will certainly keep your pants up."

The mayor seems to evaporate from the stage the moment the cameras stop rolling.

Two hours later, at noon, Søren traverses three times along a six-block stretch of Main Street. The vibes of North River seep into his artistic soul, and he observes the nuances of color and light playing across the local storefronts, paying particular attention to the New Amsterdam and Larry's Liquor. Three cars drift out of the traffic in unison and park directly in front of Larry's.

Søren checks his watch. "Perfect timing," he says to himself. During an excursion the day before, he determined that 1:30 p.m. was the ideal time for his shoot. The three cars only needed to stay parked for ninety minutes, well within the two-hour parking limit.

Søren believes the early afternoon sun will produce deep, thin shadows around the storefront frames, creating a three-dimensional effect to make the buildings pop out during his shoot. He casts a glance at the beautifully cloudless sky.

Søren's film crew arrives in front of the New Amsterdam at 12:45 p.m. Jake, the lead cameraman, hops out and introduces his soundman, Daniel, and their assistant, Glenda. Jake and Søren have collaborated on several projects, and Jake is doing the shoot pro bono as a campaign contribution to Maggie. Previously Jake ran point on a documentary of the Free the Bees movement.

As the three unload the van, Søren steps into the New Amsterdam to chat with Grant, who assures him that the street crowd is assembling as they speak. Several dozen of Grant's customers had volunteered.

"One thirty, Grant. That's when we roll the cameras."

Grant responds with a thumbs-up.

Back outside, Jake hands Søren a second camera, and they test and tune the equipment. Søren's main concern is the directional microphone. He and Jake cross the street and carry on a mock conversation until the soundman signals okay. After peeking around the corner of the New Amsterdam and confirming the car and trailer are ready, the film crew and

Søren make their way toward Larry's Liquor, filming and interviewing passers-by about Proposition 420.

At 1:30 p.m., the cameras are focused on Larry's Liquor. Søren films from across the street, and Jake is off to the side, capturing the sidewalk in front of the store, just out of sight of Søren's camera. On cue, Søren sees the silver Honda CR-V with its ten-foot-long trailer coming down Main Street. The CR-V slows as it approaches Larry's Liquor, allowing the three parked vehicles to depart so it can pull up at the curb in front of the store.

At the car end of the trailer is a marvelous papier-mâché re-creation of Rodin's bronze statue, *The Thinker.* The painted figure, seated on a stone with his head resting on a bent arm, is staring downward at a giant doobie at the rear end of the trailer. The tip of the papier-mâché joint glows slightly red, and an occasional wisp of smoke pops out and floats away in the breeze. Standing beside the mammoth doobie is a life-size mannequin dressed in a blue-and-white plaid dress, looking like a 1950s housewife. Her right arm is raised, and she is holding a sign showing the number 420 overlain by a red circle with a diagonal line through it. Beneath the entire display, along both sides of the trailer, are banners that read *Vote No on Proposition 420.*

Grant's crowd of onlookers gathers on the sidewalk around the display. Søren zooms in ever so slightly and captures Larry's employees in the front window; some are smiling, and others are laughing and pointing—an unexpected bonus. Fortuitously they have positioned themselves directly below the words *Larry's Liquor* painted on the shop window. His only disappointment is that the microphone can't pick up the laughter through the glass. One person in the back disappears into the rear of the store.

Søren holds his breath momentarily, wondering if the gods of good fortune are smiling in his direction on this glorious day. Perhaps, he thinks, the cosmic roulette wheel will land on his number. He hears that little white ball bouncing around as the wheel spins. Out of the shadows in the back of the store emerges the face of Larry Oligard.

Søren steadies himself and whispers into his open line with the crew, "Here comes the action. Don't miss it."

Larry exits the store with a dangerously sour look on his face. He makes a beeline for the CR-V, whose passenger window is rolled down. "What the hell are you doing? You can't park this thing in front of my store."

The driver rolls up the passenger window as he speaks: "Public parking, dude. I've got another hour and fifty-five minutes on the clock."

Larry bangs on the window and repeats his message.

Somewhere, a voice hollers out, "Liquor kills you quicker."

Larry swirls around, taking in the size of the crowd in front of his store for the first time. "Crap! Just my luck. A bunch of potheads."

The soundman signals he captured the outburst.

Larry paces for a moment before walking to the back of the trailer. He uses the wheel-well cover to step up closer to the mannequin and her sign. The arms weren't flexible enough to reach skyward when Søren constructed the float, so he had to saw off the right arm and glue it back in place with the sign pole discreetly bolted to the mannequin's hand. Her dress covered the sloppy glue work. As Larry tugs on the sign, the arm breaks off at the shoulder. Larry stumbles backward and has to drop the arm to avoid falling. The red glue makes it look like a bloody stump.

"Oh my God. He's killing her!" shouts one of the bystanders.

"It's a mannequin, you idiots. You can't kill her," retorts Larry as he picks the arm up off the sidewalk.

He turns to face the crowd as several screams erupt. "He's armed and dangerous. Run!"

The crowd surges away from Larry, and Jake repositions himself nearer to the curb to catch the action.

Larry turns his back on the crowd, shaking his head. He raises the arm, which still holds the bolted-on sign, steps up onto the wheel well cover, and tries to reattach it to the mannequin. As he waves the sign high in the air, people stop moving, and a woman close to Larry shouts: "Wait a minute, he's waving the sign. He's one of us. He's joining the cause." A chant of "No to 420" starts up. Larry shakes his head again.

It is only when he tries one last time to connect the arm to its rightful owner that he notices Søren across the street. "Hey, you. Stop taking pictures." Larry starts bobbing the sign up and down to use it as a pointer while he shouts. "You can't film me. It's an invasion of my privacy."

Søren waves at Larry with his free hand. "Don't worry, Mr. Oligard, I have a city permit to film this afternoon. It's all cool."

Larry blows a fuse and starts beating the giant doobie with the bloody arm stump. Every time he smacks it, a large puff of smoke shoots out of the red tip. The crowd changes its chant to "Toke it again, Larry, toke it again."

Larry finally stops when the arm breaks through the papier-mâché and becomes wedged in the top of the doobie with the No-420 sign still proudly on display. Søren stops filming after Larry's shoulders slump, and he shuffles back into the store.

The Thinker dispassionately looks on, contemplating the true meaning of a one-armed mannequin watching a mega-joint hold her arm and protest against Proposition 420.

After consulting with Melonie and Maggie, Søren releases some of the raw footage to North River News. Full disclosure of the circumstances surrounding the incident is made, along with information that the police were called to the scene after the fact.

Søren knocks on Melonie's door at 5:50 p.m. Thaddeus greets him and points out Road to Buddha's Farm as they head to the kitchen.

"Nice," Søren says.

With a round of cold IPAs they sit in the living room to watch the six o'clock news.

"This is Connie Carter bringing you the latest North River news. The election battle is heating up. This morning Mayor John Harper and his opponent, Maggie Harper, his older sister, appeared on the morning show to discuss their views on Proposition 420. The mayor supports it on community safety grounds, and Maggie Harper opposes it as an infringement on free enterprise."

The program cuts to comments from both candidates and ends with Maggie saying, "By the way, brother, I like the look of your new suspenders. Those babies will certainly keep your pants up."

"We believe this was a reference to the incident several weeks ago, when Maggie pantsed her brother," says Connie. A shot of the mayor's green Dr. Seuss boxer shorts appears behind her.

"More Proposition 420 news broke this afternoon when Maggie Harper's campaign was filming a political ad on Main Street. Allegedly, liquor store owner Larry Oligard ran from his store and attacked the production props used in the filming. He assaulted a mannequin, ripping her arm off and using it to beat a large papier-mâché marijuana cigarette." Footage of the incident silently plays as Connie speaks. Larry's vigorous attack on the giant doobie is captured in its entirety, and the clip ends with Larry standing over the smoking joint with the arm and the attached No-420 sign held high.

"The campaign's artistic director, Søren, a local North River artist whose work is on display at the Fine Arts Museum, speaks with North River News reporter Erika Cool about the incident."

The screen flips to Erika standing in Søren's studio. "Thank you, Connie. I'm coming to you from the art studio of Søren. Søren, can you shed any light on the cause of Mr. Oligard's attack."

The camera pans to Søren in front of a wall-size blowup of Larry holding the No-420 sign, with the doobie coming up to about crotch level and a large puff of smoke exiting the tip. "Honestly, Erika, I think

Larry was just having a bad day. Despite our set being vandalized, we are declining to press charges, and Maggie Harper's campaign wishes him a speedy recovery."

"Was Mr. Oligard injured in the attack?"

"No, Erika, not to my knowledge. But there was clearly some sort of psychotic break in play. Although, by the end, we wondered if he had a change of heart when he started waving the No-420 sign in the air. Perhaps if you interview Larry, he might give you more insight."

The camera swings back to Erika. "We contacted Mr. Oligard, but he declined to comment. Before we leave, could you let our viewers know why you go by the single name of Søren?"

"Sure, Erika. Søren is actually my real first name. I'm named after the Danish philosopher Søren Kierkegaard. Early in my career, during my urban cityscape phase, I wanted a simple way for people to associate my name with my art. So, I legally changed my full name to just Søren. "

"Thank you, Søren. And now, back to you, Connie."

Thaddeus lowers the sound on the television, looks to Søren, and raises a glass of IPA. "Well done!"

Franky

Maggie was polling well the week after Søren's first ad aired. The North River News coverage had inspired a flood of small donor contributions to the campaign, and Maggie's army of gray-haired canvassers knocked on plenty of doors across the city. Mable and Adele had taken to marching daily in front of city hall with signs saying *Pants the Mayor by Voting for Maggie*. Their signs each had a picture of the mayor's green boxers, and Mable had taken care to dye her hair the exact same shade of emerald. They even made the six o'clock news with a picture of the mayor leaving work, with the two campaign signs in the background.

Between her day job and her side gig as Maggie's campaign manager, Melonie was booked from the moment she rolled out of bed in the morning to when she collapsed in the evening. Thaddeus used his expanded free time wisely by working longer hours at the botanical gardens, happily indulging in his horticultural obsessions.

The week had started poorly. He arrived at the gardens on Monday just before seven to find a dozen of his best clematis missing. Unlike the last incident, they had been dug out by the roots leaving deep holes in the moist black soil. These were specialty varieties he had ordered and planted only a week ago. Then this morning, he discovered three bonsai trees were missing: a twenty-seven-year-old Japanese white pine, a thirty-six-year-old atropurpureum maple, and a forty-five-year-old Shimpaku juniper.

A red brick partially covered an envelope right where the Shimpaku juniper had once been. Thaddeus pulled the envelope out. It was sealed with a dark crimson wax that had a stamped signet-ring impression of three jonquils. He carefully opened it and read the note: *We need to talk if you want to see your plants again. Meet me at the park bench on the west side of the Arch Bridge.*

Thaddeus thought it odd that no day or time was mentioned, but as he looked back down at the brick, he saw the corner of another piece of paper and unfolded it. *Sorry for the confusion. I forgot to say the meeting will be on Friday at noon—this Friday, assuming you get the note by then. I'm writing you late Wednesday night. Have a nice day.*

Thaddeus pocketed the notes and strolled back to greenhouse 9, thinking about the chain of events. Who knew what was at stake: money, illegal favors, season passes to the botanical gardens? Whatever the outcome, Thaddeus was intrigued and looking forward to tomorrow's meeting.

....

(Present)

Thaddeus arrives early at the Arch Bridge and takes a seat on the bench, which commands a marvelous view overlooking the river. Thaddeus gazes upriver and can barely make out the Devil Woods Dam and Anubis's final resting place. A light breeze blows from the south, and he shuts his eyes, feeling the radiance of the sun on his face and taking in the damp organic smells wafting from the riverbank.

After a few minutes, he registers some shuffling beside him and feels someone sitting on the other end of the bench. He opens his eyes and, to his left, sees a big fellow fidgeting nervously and almost looking apologetic. Thaddeus eyes him, saying nothing. He takes another hard look and thinks he knows the guy from somewhere but can't quite place him.

"Mr. Barcelona, thank you for meeting me, and I'm sorry for the unfortunate nature of our business. But still, it is a very pleasant day. Have you ever noticed how the water grass in the river shallows wiggles with the current? You can see it when the water's clear, like today."

Thaddeus looks down at the base of the bridge and observes the rippling water grass. He is a little unsettled about this clandestine meeting, but he keeps the conversation cordial "You picked a nice spot to meet, Mr...?"

"Oh, you can call me Franky. I'm like a ghost, though; you will never be able to find my last name or where I live. So don't even try."

"Okay, Franky. And by the way, call me Thaddeus. So what do we need to talk about today?"

"Well, Mr. Barcelona—I mean Thaddeus—you probably know I have some very special plants of yours. But I don't want you to worry. I have repotted all of the clematises and have them resting in partial sun. They're getting plenty of water each day since it's a little on the warm and dry side. Oh, I took the liberty of adding a small bit of fertilizer to each pot since it's the right season to give them some nutritional encouragement. Also, I'm watering the bonsais each morning and doing a late afternoon check to ensure the soil doesn't dry out. I saw you had recently pruned a medium-sized branch on the white pine, so I've made sure the antiseptic paste stays firmly attached to the wound."

"You seem to know a lot about plants, Franky. I'm impressed."

"I love plants. I find them nicer than most people I meet. Several years back, before that nasty pandemic, I worked as a landscaper. But things shut down while everyone was sick, and I had to find new employment."

Sparks fly in his brain, and Thaddeus places Franky's face. He saw him once at Jackson's Nursery and Landscapes. It was well over five years ago when Thaddeus was at Jackson's arranging services for the botanical gardens. Franky was on one of their work crews. Thaddeus had watched from the office window while Franky and two other guys loaded up a truck with plants for a residential landscaping project. Thaddeus filed that information away for future consideration.

"By the way, I apologize for my original disturbance when I dug up your clematis garden. I was interrupted partway through and had to leave the uprooted plants. Also, sorry about the three broken stalks."

"Don't worry. I'm nursing those back to health. They'll be fine. But perhaps you should tell me why we are here today."

Franky hesitates for a moment. "It's not a pleasant piece of business, Thaddeus. My employer wants you to do something for him before I return the plants. Obviously, I can't tell you who my employer is."

"You mean you're holding my plants hostage in exchange for a favor?"

"I don't like to think of this as a hostage situation. I'm just trying to get your attention." Franky stares at the ground for a moment, looking despondent about the whole affair.

"What's the favor? I can't make any promises regarding the botanical gardens."

"No, no. It's nothing like that. You see, my employer wants your girlfriend to stop asking questions about the north bank development. He thinks the southeastern end of the riverbank is ideal for planting lots of trees, and she should focus her efforts there. But this negotiation of ours has nothing to do with Condo Carl. He knows nothing about it."

"Interesting" is all Thaddeus could say. He pulls a Gaia Gold from his vest pocket, lights it up, takes a long drag, then passes it to Franky. Franky tokes a bit and hands it back. The two men sit in silence for several minutes.

Franky settles back into his seat, looking relaxed and laid back. "Not bad stuff, boss."

"It's my own brand. I produced the plants and got them patented a while ago."

"You're a plant genius, Thaddeus. I've got to hand it to you. So, what do you think about the proposal?"

"Quite honestly, Franky, I don't think it's possible. Melonie doesn't like to be told what to do. I'm sure she'd tell your employer to stick his proposal where the sun don't shine."

"I hear you, Thaddeus. My missus doesn't listen to a word I say. That woman is damn well going to do what she wants to. My daughter is only six, and she's picking up the vibes from her mom. She's going to be just as hard-headed one day."

"I'll tell you what, Franky. I'm not too worried about the plants because you're taking great care of them, and I trust you to keep them healthy."

"Thanks, boss."

"But I eventually have to get them back. Tell your employer I would be happy to negotiate about something else."

"What do you mean 'negotiate about something else'? I don't think that's how this type of transaction is supposed to work."

"It just makes sense, Franky. I want the plants back, and he wants to negotiate. Melonie's not going to negotiate about trying to stop the development—she doesn't care about the plants as much as I do. So, since we're all sensible people, it's clear we need to negotiate about something else."

Franky thinks about the proposition. "Like what?"

"It's a good question. I don't know. Do you have any ideas? I don't know him."

"It's a tough one, Thaddeus. He runs a few nightclubs where I occasionally work as a bouncer, but he doesn't need any favors in that area."

Thaddeus nods and looks out over the river from their semi-secluded spot. "Let's walk back to the gardens while I think things over. Maybe I could get your opinion on some of my projects as we stroll through the gardens."

They finish off the Gaia Gold before leaving.

Thaddeus and Franky return to the botanical gardens and wander to the northwest quadrant, where Thaddeus has been working on the conifer collection. The two spend about an hour discussing some problems he's encountered. Much to Thaddeus's satisfaction, Franky offers a wealth of excellent advice. This gets him thinking about a movie he once saw where an enemy spy was craftily turned into a double agent.

They return to the rear of greenhouse 9 and sit in two folding aluminum lawn chairs. Thaddeus takes the one with the rotting straps and gives the other to Franky.

"I've been thinking about our negotiations," says Thaddeus. "You mentioned your employer wanted two things: stopping the campaign against the development and planting trees at the southeastern end of the riverbank."

"Yes, Mr. CRJ—crap, I didn't mean to say his name."

"It's okay, Franky. I know Sergei is a Russian name, but I don't know anyone who goes by it."

Franky momentarily considers the exchange and plows ahead. "My employer knows nothing about landscaping, but for some reason, he wants a shitload of trees planted there."

"Well, I'd be willing to ask Melonie about restoring the habitats in that area. She has mentioned the need for tree groves several times."

Franky checks his watch. "That might work. I'll suggest it to him. But I have to leave now, boss. I got a downtown bouncer job tonight, and I need to get home and have dinner with my wife and daughter. My mamma and daddy always ate dinner with the whole family, so I try and make sure I'm there each evening at dinner for my little girl. It doesn't hurt that my missus is the best Italian cook in the city."

"I don't want to keep you, but I've got one last thing for you to think about. I recently got approval to hire another gardener. How about you come and work for me here?"

It takes Franky a moment to find his voice. "What? Work here, with the plants, full-time?"

Thaddeus nods. "I don't know what your current employer pays, but the salary for the position is decent. Plus, you get benefits—healthcare and retirement—and a nine-to-five work schedule, so you're home every day for dinner with your daughter. You might even be able to quit the bouncer work."

Franky says he'll think about the job, but Thaddeus knows from the look on his face he has already accepted it. "Let me know by the end of next week, Franky. Also let me know if your employer will accept my proposal."

Who the hell is Sergei? Wonders Thaddeus as Franky walks out of greenhouse 9.

When Thaddeus arrives at Melonie's condo an hour later, he is still contemplating the events of the afternoon. He doesn't want to distract her—she has enough on her plate—but he needs information. She has half an hour before a planning session with Søren, so they sit on her balcony to relax with a glass of wine.

Thaddeus waits until their glasses are half empty before making conversation. "Are you and Søren starting to campaign against the north bank development or still focusing on Proposition 420?"

"That's what we need to decide this evening."

"What's the story behind it? Is it just politics as usual, or is Condo Carl some sort of organized crime guy?" Thaddeus knows that Melonie has spent a good deal of time researching Condo Carl and the deal he and Mayor John are dreaming up.

"Carl Blankers is just another asshole developer who thinks climate change is a hoax and the manifest destiny of builders is to pave over as much of the world as possible. Money is the first consideration in everything he does. The bond initiative on the ballot is a scheme to have taxpayers pick up a considerable chunk of the cost for his new development. Luxury condo buyers will profit, but what the city really needs more of is affordable housing, not million-dollar condominiums. I wouldn't be surprised if Carl's books and tax returns stretch the bounds of reasonable legal practices, but I haven't seen anything in my research connecting him to organized crime."

Thaddeus silently considers Melonie's assessment.

"Now, Carl Jr. is another matter. I wouldn't put anything past that little twerp. He runs an industrial-waste disposal company that his grandfather started. Several times in the past three or four years, we've had illegal dumping of hazardous waste onto public lands. His company was suspected in two of the cases, but nothing could be proven. He also runs some sleazy nightclubs uptown in the northwest district. I've been told they're thinly disguised strip clubs."

The tumblers are starting to click in Thaddeus's mind.

Melonie continues: "Carl Jr. is convinced his dad will pass the family real estate business onto him one day. He has publicly bragged about it, but I think he's deluding himself. He may be the eldest child, but his younger sister, Brittany, inherited the brains. Carl Jr. has screwed up every real estate deal he's ever been involved in. Brittany, on the other hand, is the company's chief financial officer. My money is on the baby girl being the next CEO when Daddy steps down."

Melonie pauses to take a sip of chardonnay.

"What's Carl's middle name?" asks Thaddeus.

Over the top of her wineglass, Melonie shifts her hazel-green eyes to him. Thaddeus understands it is her "What are you up to?" look. "Ronald. Why do you ask?"

His mind flips back and forth several times: Sergei, Carl Ronald Junior, Sergei, CRJ. The connection stabilizes. "No real reason. Just curiosity."

Melonie looks at her watch. "I have to get online with Søren, but when I finish with this meeting, I want to hear what you're up to." She flashes him a smile as she slips through the door into the living room. His heart melts, as always.

Thaddeus searches on his phone for information about the southeast riverbank land Franky mentioned. After fifteen minutes of reading, more pieces of the puzzle fall into place. Until five years ago, the area was an active landfill. But when environmental surveys showed significant leakage from buried waste seeping into the river, federal regulators closed down the operation. A drainage curtain was sunk into the bedrock to prevent further contamination of the river. Then the whole site was leveled off with a layer of topsoil and methane vents were installed. The land has lain fallow since then and is currently covered with weeds, grasses, and brambles. But that clearly isn't enough for Carl Jr. He wants a forest on the site. *Why?* Wonders Thaddeus.

Buried Below

Thaddeus's instincts were correct; Franky applied for the job on Monday morning. On Tuesday, he reported for his first day of work with six clematis and three bonsais carefully packed in the back of his cherry-red pickup truck. Thaddeus helped him unload and inquired if Franky's former employer had agreed to the proposal.

"He did, boss. But, I'll tell you, he wasn't happy when I quit. He pulled out my contract and kept pointing to something called a nondisclosure agreement. I wasn't sure what that was all about, but I told him I would rather work with plants than people. He shook his head, gave me last week's paycheck, and wished me luck. According to him, I'm not supposed to discuss anything that happened when I was working for him. I might get sued if I do."

"Well, you're here on the job, and the plants are back safe and sound. So there is nothing to talk about concerning your former job as far as I'm concerned."

"Oh yeah, boss. He sent you a map showing where he wants the trees planted and offered to pay for them as a memorial to his grandfather. "

Franky handed Thaddeus a map of the abandoned landfill on the southeastern riverbank. He had circled an area in red and written trees inside it. Thaddeus considered that Carl Jr. may have the most inept criminal mind he had ever encountered.

"Well, he seems to know just where he wants the grove of trees," said Thaddeus.

Franky looked around and lowered his voice. "One night, when I was working at the Golden Girl, I heard some of his boys talking. They had drunk too much beer, and their tongues were loose and waggling. One of them kept going on about something being buried out there by the river." He took a second look around.

"Interesting. But I didn't hear it from you, Franky. I respect your nondisclosure agreement."

Franky smiled. "I'm gonna like working for you, Thaddeus."

"Let's discuss your first project."

Thaddeus pointed to a walkway, where the two made their way to the north edge of the grounds. The gardens extended to the river and occupied the south bank directly opposite the contentious north bank development.

They stood on a large rock at the river's edge. Thaddeus spread his arms wide to indicate the entire river bank. "Use your imagination, Franky. Envision this stretch of the botanical gardens along the riverbank, planted with only native plant species. We design it with subtle, unobtrusive walking paths where a person can explore the riparian ecosystem and feel like they're a part of it. They can get a taste of the natural riverbank ecology."

"Are you thinking free-flowing or more stylized, like a Japanese garden?" asked Franky.

"The question is not what I'm thinking—what are you thinking? This is your project. You get the first shot at the design concept. Spend the day walking the riverbank, checking out the nooks and crannies. Do some reading on native plants. Put a conceptual plan together."

"Very cool, boss."

Franky's attention wandered to the far bank. "Hey, isn't that your girlfriend and that artist guy from the news?"

Thaddeus waved both hands until Søren spotted him and tapped Melonie on the shoulder. The two walked over to the edge, but the river was too wide to effectively have a conversation. Melonie called him from her cell, and both switched to speaker mode.

"Søren, how are you?" asked Thaddeus.

"Life is treating me well as always, Thaddeus. Melonie and I are scouting the area for the Rescue the River Rally in two weeks. We've already filed for a permit with the city. It'll be the campaign kickoff to oppose the North Bank Development Bond. The working slogan is 'Say No to Mayor John's Bondage Fetish.'"

Melonie chimed in: "Jill Jammin is composing a new piece for the rally called 'The Beast of Bondage.'"

"I can't wait to hear it," said Thaddeus. "Franky, here, is the new gardener we hired yesterday. We were just discussing our restoration of the south bank along the stretch owned by the botanical gardens. After we brainstorm, we'll have a sit-down with the city planning team. A well-coordinated effort—that's the name of the game."

Melonie gave them a thumbs-up from across the river, then she and Søren returned to their planning.

"My wife is a big Jill Jammin fan," said Franky. "She's gonna want to go to that rally."

"Since Melonie is Maggie's campaign manager, I'm sure I'll be there too. All right, Franky, you start thinking about our restoration project. I need to get back for a meeting with the director. Let's talk tomorrow morning over a cup of coffee. I might be leaving mid-afternoon to go across the river and look at this area where your former employer wants the tree grove."

"It's pretty isolated over there, Thaddeus. There are also some pretty rough characters living in the abandoned office of the old landfill. It might not be too safe."

"I'll be fine, Franky."

....

(Present)

Thaddeus arrives at the entrance to the defunct landfill on his new Dorsal Eighteen electric scooter. The gates are locked, but he notices a gaping hole he can crawl through between the two silver chainlink front gate panels. Thaddeus has a large black bag with shoulder straps attached to his back. He locks the scooter, slips off the bag, carefully unzips it, and extracts a yellow magnetic locator. The device is shaped like a laser weapon from a Star Wars episode, with a pistol grip and readout display on the back end. He had paid a little under $1,000 for the MagnoFinder in hopes that it would help him solve the mystery of Carl Jr.'s sudden interest in planting trees.

The company's website said it would detect large metal objects, like waste disposal drums. He had practiced on some spots in the gardens where he knew metal objects were buried, and he successfully located them. He isn't sure it will do what he needs, but it seems worth a try.

Thaddeus pushes the magnetic locator through the hole in the gates and squeezes in behind it; then, he consults his map. The map is a combination of Google Maps, aerial photos, and Carl Jr.'s hand-drawn circle showing where he wants the trees planted. It also indicates the location of the buildings that once served as offices for landfill operations. His inner voice tells him it's best to take Franky's advice and avoid the deserted buildings.

The main road loops around by the original offices, but the aerial photo shows a walking path cutting directly to the river and intersecting the landfill area Little Carl circled. Small trees and low shrubs hide the path from the abandoned offices. Thaddeus arrives at his destination in five minutes.

He is excited about testing the MagnoFinder. It's a cool little device, and he can't resist dropping to one knee and pretending to fire it like

70

a space-age pistol. After a stroll around the area, he gets to work using orange and blue flags with thin, short wire poles to mark rows on the east and west ends of the investigation area. The flags are three feet apart, and Thaddeus uses them as guides while walking back and forth along the rows, roughly marking the spots on his paper map where large metal objects are detected. He works his way from north to south, taking just over ninety minutes to complete the survey.

Slowly the map takes form: a rectangle eighteen feet wide and thirty-six feet long in the center of the survey area. He runs a few diagonal traverses to confirm the boundaries of the buried metal.

He's finishing up when he hears a voice behind him: "Hey, you. What are you doing?"

Thaddeus turns to find three scraggly-looking men standing at the head of the footpath where he had walked in. They are all close to his size, and the one doing the talking wears a black nylon windbreaker with holes in the elbows. About a week's worth of black-and-gray stubble covers his chin, and a red bandanna keeps an untamed mop of grayish hair out of his face. The thin man on his right has a tan coat with sleeves too long for his arms, and the guy next to him leans on a two-by-four the length of a baseball bat.

They approach and stop at the northern boundary of the rectangle, with Thaddeus on the southern end. He is struck by the symmetry, with the two parties standing opposite each other with a mass of buried metal between them. He wonders if it has any cosmic significance.

"Hey, we asked you what you're doing," says the skinny guy in the tan coat.

"I'm doing a little investigation to see what's under the ground here."

"Well, this is our territory," says Red Bandanna with a malicious smirk. "If you want to do anything here, it'll cost you." Babe Ruth lifts the two-by-four off the ground and Skinny Guy gives a nervous glance over his shoulder.

Thaddeus is slightly worried but pissed off at their attitude. "It's public land, my friends. You don't own anything."

"There're three of us who say it's ours. How much money do you have on you?" Red Bandanna offers his ugly smile again.

Thaddeus shifts position slightly, holding the MagnoFinder by the pistol grip and pointing it at the ground. "I don't think you want to go there. Do you know what I have in my hand?" He lifts the locator and waves the yellow barrel in a small circle. The three men remain silent, but Skinny Guy fidgets and keeps looking over his shoulder.

"This is a ground-penetrating laser pistol. Believe me, if it can penetrate eighteen feet underground, it can fry your worthless asses. Your insides will be burnt hamburger." Thaddeus points the locator at the ground directly in front of him.

"You're bluffing," says Red Bandanna after a pause. The skinny man shuffles his feet back and forth. Babe Ruth puts the tip of his makeshift bat back on the ground and eyes the magnetic locator.

"Maybe," says Thaddeus. "Maybe not."

Red Bandanna takes a step forward, but his buddies remain still. "Come on, you pussies. The man is not out here with some military-grade space-age laser." He squints at Thaddeus. "We were just going to take your money. But now we'll have to give you a good beating too."

Thaddeus responds by lifting the barrel of the magnetic locator up across his chest and gripping it with his left hand.

The men pause momentarily before walking forward and spreading out a bit to hem Thaddeus in. Thaddeus, thankful for four years of weekly Aikido classes, decides on a systematic approach. He waits until they're five feet away, then swings the barrel of the MagnoFinder toward Skinny Guy and makes a loud buzzing noise in the back of his throat. The man screams and throws his arms up to block his face as Thaddeus rushes him. Thaddeus manages to poke him once with the barrel before he drops the weapon and grabs the man's jacket lapel with his right hand and his wrist with his left. He executes a perfect twist-and-throw, sending the guy flying through the air. He hears the arm crack as the man hits the ground and lets go of another squeaky scream.

Red Bandanna throws a punch just as Thaddeus pivots left and slides backward. He manages to grip the palm of Red Bandanna's hand just above the wrist and twists it into a painful wrist lock. He does his best to maneuver Red Bandanna in between him and the third guy, but he's not quick enough, and the flat side of the two-by-four catches him squarely in the back. Thaddeus stumbles forward onto his left knee, and the two men are immediately on him, pinning him to the ground.

The fight has not gone as well as he had hoped. With only ten dollars in his pocket, he contemplates negotiating but figures he will take a beating no matter what. Before he gets too far into a new plan, the weight on his back lifts, and he scrambles to his feet to see Franky holding each of the men by their collars. They are on their toes, barely touching the ground. He shoves Red Bandanna one way and Babe Ruth the other. A swift kick in the ass from Franky sends Babe to his knees.

"Whatever you gentlemen are thinking about doing, don't. It won't go well for you." Skinny Guy is moaning and cradling his arm. "I realize you men are down on your luck. But you can't be beating and robbing

Mr. B. because of your own bad fortune."

Franky has a unique way of sounding calm, sincere, and threatening at the same time.

"Here's what we are going to do," he continues. "I'm going to put twenty dollars for each of you on the ground so you can get a decent meal and calm down. You"—he points to Skinny Guy—"should go to the Fourteenth Street Clinic and let them set that arm for free. You're lucky Mr. B. wasn't trying to really hurt you. He and I are going to leave here, and you won't be following us."

Franky picks up the two-by-four and tosses it toward the river before snatching up the MagnoFinder. He points Thaddeus up the trail and follows with a side-stepping walk that lets him keep an eye on the men.

Once they round the bend and are out of sight, he says, "Not bad, boss. I thought you had them for a while."

"You saw the whole thing?"

"Yeah. I followed you over here—it's not a safe place."

"Why didn't you step in earlier?"

"I have a policy of not messing with other people's business unless I have to. Particularly if I haven't been invited. Like I said, you might have handled the whole thing yourself."

Thaddeus rubs his chin and thinks about the irony of a former blackmailer becoming the rescuer. "I see what you mean, Franky. I should have taken your advice."

"That's okay. My mom used to say, 'Live and learn.'"

"Were you really going to fry them into hamburgers with this thing?" asks Franky as he waves the barrel of the yellow magnetic locator.

"No, you couldn't fry an ant with that."

Franky chuckles. "I didn't think so. Did you find anything with your investigation?"

"Nothing you should know about. Not with your nondisclosure problem."

Franky says nothing.

When they arrive at the front gate, Thaddeus sees the hole is now much larger, just about the size needed for Franky to fit through.

"Let's put your scooter in the bed of my truck, and I'll drive you back to the botanical gardens."

"Sounds like a plan. How about we stop at the Pearl, and I buy you a beer?"

"I'll have to take a raincheck, Thaddeus. My daughter, Carmen, is in a show tonight at school, and I don't want to miss that. They grow up fast, you know."

"You've got your priorities in order, Franky. Drop me off at the front gates and enjoy the show. I want to hear about it tomorrow morning."

"Sure thing, boss."

Rescue the River

The Rescue the River Rally was approaching. Melonie and Søren had worked madly for the past nine days, tending to a long list of logistical preparations, but the stars were now aligning. Their biggest concern was crowd size; they estimated 500 with a maximum of 1,500. But it was difficult to feel confident in the numbers. The rally was scheduled to start the next day at 4:00 p.m. Protesters would gather at the botanical gardens and proceed to Main Street. After several more blocks of marching, they would cross the Pearl Street Bridge to North Bank Boulevard, where a dead-end side street provided access to the riverside site of the north bank development project.

Søren calculated the march would take sixty minutes for a crowd of 500 and about ninety minutes for a crowd of 1,500. Traffic-control police officers and a motorcycle escort to keep people on the sidewalks had been part of the event permit. Fortunately, the Pearl Street Bridge had a spacious walkway with ample guard rails to protect pedestrians from traffic.

Melonie had timed the protest march to make it onto the evening news, with coverage of Jill Jammin's sunset concert hopefully being broadcast the next day. She hoped Erika Cool would cover the march.

Food and drink provisions included three beer stands, courtesy of the Pearl Bridge Bar, and nine food trucks stationed around the concert area. The single biggest logistical operation for the rally had been constructing a temporary stage for Jill's debut of "The Beast of Bondage."

The organizational team had started hyping the rally several weeks before, using social media, paper flyers, and volunteer phone trees. Mother Nature also cooperated with a forecast of 70 degrees and a cloudless sky. The rallying slogan, *Say No to Mayor John's Bondage Fetish*, was popping up in online postings and on storefront banners. The mayor had kept a low profile.

The team started running spots on the radio and local TV three days ago. "The people of North River enjoy one of the most beautiful cities in the country. Our botanical gardens on the treasured banks of the North River are internationally acclaimed. Do you really want to pay additional taxes to fund luxury condominiums? Housing that provides only the wealthy with access to our scenic riverbanks? Vote no on the North Bank Development Bond and vote yes for Maggie Harper, our next mayor."

....

(Present)

A crowd starts gathering at three in the afternoon. By 3:30 p.m., the parking lot in front of the botanical gardens is packed, and people are still arriving. A festive mood is in the air, and hundreds of signs are bobbing over the crowd, reminding people to *say no to Mayor John's bondage fetish and to vote for Maggie!*

Thaddeus leaves greenhouse 9 to join the protesters in front and hears the murmur of the crowd. He takes a detour through the new clematis garden to inspect the vines and arrives at the front gates at four o'clock.

He searches for several minutes through the thick of the crowd before finding Grant, who has volunteered to help with the march. "Quite the crowd we have today, Grant."

"I am super excited about the turnout. We're now estimating about two thousand, so our original estimates were low. I think our advertising for the rally was perfect."

"Does Melonie know?"

"I just called her. They're adjusting the schedule on their end to accommodate a slightly longer march."

"Is there anything I can do?"

"You could walk with me. Søren and Maggie will be up there," Grant points toward the front gate, "and I could use some help at the tail end to keep things moving forward."

Thaddeus nods, but before he can say yes, someone taps his shoulder. He turns to face a camera crew and Erika Cool's smiling face.

"Thaddeus, would you do a two-minute interview for us?"

He's not keen on public interviews but knows he doesn't really have a choice since Melonie is one of the organizers, and he is a representative of the botanical gardens. "Sure, Erika."

She positions him to catch the size of the crowd in the background. "This is Erika Cool with North River News, bringing you our coverage of the Rescue the River rally organized by mayoral candidate Maggie Harper. People are protesting the luxury condo project on the river's north bank, directly across from the botanical gardens. We are in front of the North River Botanical Gardens now, where the march will soon start. The crowd you see will walk from the south bank to the north bank,

76

where the rally will take place. We are here with Thaddeus Barcelona, the garden's curator. Mr. Barcelona, what do you think of the north bank development project?"

"Thanks for interviewing me, Erika. The botanical gardens are run by the city, and, as per city policy, we don't take official positions on ballot measures. But I can tell you that at our garden, we're planning to restore the entire length of the riverbank that borders our property. The restoration is a big one, and we will integrate native species into a brand-new riverside ecological zone. We are very excited about the project. Our restoration plans stand in stark contrast to the concrete boardwalk proposed by the North Bank Development Bond. As an individual, I will be voting no on the bond."

"Mr. Barcelona, your work with the botanical gardens has brought international acclaim to our city. Tell us why you oppose a boardwalk where people can be right next to the water."

"There is no question that an extensive boardwalk will allow people to experience the water close up, but the river is more than just water. It is a beautiful ecosystem, where hundreds of aquatic and land species mingle. The replacement of the plant border along the riverbank with concrete will take away valuable spawning grounds for fish and will also deprive many species of necessary food sources. The boardwalk gets you close to the water but farther away from the beauty of the river system itself."

"Thank you, Mr. Barcelona. North River News contacted the mayor about the environmental concerns raised by this protest rally, but his office declined to comment."

Erika signs off and points her crew in the direction of Maggie, who she has just spotted. Grant and Thaddeus watch as Søren organizes the front of the crowd to start the march. Thaddeus sees Franky and gives him a wave. He and his family walk over.

"Thaddeus, this is my wife, Catherine, and our daughter, Carmen."

"It's a pleasure to meet you, Thaddeus," says Franky's wife. "Most people just call me Cat. I wanted to thank you personally for giving Franky a job at the botanical gardens. It's his dream job." Franky rolls his eyes. "I'm also glad he's not working for that little weasel Carl. He's one bad apple."

"Mommy, you always say name calling's not good."

"You're right, honey. I apologize. But I'm still glad Daddy doesn't work for Mr. Carl."

Thaddeus smiles and changes the subject. "Franky tells me you're a Jill Jammin fan."

"Absolutely. I was thrilled when he told me she'd be performing tonight."

"Well, I think she's roped JoJo into playing too."

"No shit!"

"Mom, that's a bad word."

"Sorry, honey. I thought JoJo had sworn off playing live and was just into studio work. I haven't seen him play in over five years."

"Evidently, he's had a breakthrough in his subsonic bass work, and he's keen to perform. It doesn't hurt that he's also an avid supporter of the riverfront restoration."

JoJo's life work has focused on developing a branch of music called subsonic bass, where he plays the bass below the auditory threshold of most humans. The audience experiences the music by feeling it. Rumor has it that JoJo's elaborated recording studio is funded by family money, but Thaddeus knows he has some major entertainment clients.

"This is gonna be so cool," says Cat.

Organizers are working their way through the crowd, ushering the marchers toward the front gate. Thaddeus and Grant are the last to leave. Grant, using his rally sign, eases the stragglers forward.

It's 6:18 p.m. when they finally enter the rally grounds. Thaddeus can feel the electric buzz in the air. Grant buys two large cups of IPA, hands one to Thaddeus, and wanders off to mingle. Thaddeus heads toward the stage to track down Melonie and motions Franky, Cat, and Carmen to follow.

They make it backstage, where Thaddeus introduces Cat to Jill, Flower, and Harpie.

"It's a thrill to be here," says Cat. "I can't wait to hear your new piece. And look at you, woman—the pink is back."

Jill smiles and gives Cat a hug. Her pink hair tips cascade over her shoulders. "This is the first time since Anubis's departure that I've had the nerve to brighten up again."

"Yeah, I was sorry to hear about that. I read you had sworn off your pink Strat in memory of Anubis and buried it at sea with him. What are you going to play?"

"Well, a good performer has to keep some secrets. You'll have to wait and see with everyone else."

Cat laughs. "All right, I'll let you guys get to it. I'm gonna try and get close to the stage."

"I think Melonie has already arranged that for you, Cat," says Thaddeus.

Speeches are starting by the time Thaddeus and Franky's family rejoin the crowd. The department chair for the environmental science program at North River University lauds the benefits of restoring the riverbank ecosystem. This is followed by a fiery performance from the head of a local advocacy group fighting for affordable housing. Maggie is the last to speak before Jill's performance. She initially launches in with core segments from her stump speech but then drifts off to several funny stories about Little Johnny when they were growing up. People are in stitches by the time she finishes.

"But I know you didn't come here just to have your future mayor blab on about her little brother. It's all fun tonight and I think we're ready for a rocking-good performance from the one and only Jill Jammin. Are we ready?"

The crowd explodes.

"Jill wanted me to tell you she has a special guest tonight." Maggie pauses for a moment. "JoJo is back!"

They cheer, and raucous chant breaks out. "Jill, JoJo. Jill, JoJo. Jill, JoJo. Jill, JoJo..."

The sun has dipped below the horizon, and all of the lights at the rally dim except for the stage, which glows an eerie green. Five tall amplifiers stand like black towers at the back, silhouetted against the western sky. A lone figure emerges from the shadows, stopping at center stage. The spotlight comes on to reveal JoJo, standing before an array of pedals with his bass guitar slung over his right shoulder. He taps two pedals with his foot and starts playing.

An ominous feeling descends over the crowd as they feel pulsating vibrations, like the ground below is a churning basso profundo. While the audience can clearly see the five amps on stage, most are unaware of JoJo's six smaller but equally powerful amplifiers encircling the venue. However, these amps are not facing the crowd but are facing down, pumping sound energy directly into the ground. After two minutes, the sound rises to a barely audible level, but some audience members are disoriented and clinging to others for balance. One poor woman has thrown up. JoJo's weird, tactile musical style has taken them by surprise. Very slowly, some recognizable music emerges from the sonic mélange, soft and indistinct but there. JoJo builds the beat as an organized rhythm takes hold from the rumbling chaos. Harpie's bongos enter the fray, strengthening the structure of the music.

The spotlight drifts from JoJo to the back left quadrant of the stage, where Jill appears in a black jumpsuit and pink Converse high-tops. A glittering emerald-green Stratocaster twinkles as she rocks with the beat. She leans forward with a throaty whisper into the microphone: "'The

Beast of Bondage' in B, subtitle 'Penelope Jane.'"

Soft and low, she starts laying down a mournful lead with a sad G-sharp minor lilt. JoJo's sonic chaos subsides, and he nestles into a soothing audible bass below Jill's melody. Harpie's bongos slide up a notch in volume, and in the background, Flower releases long, haunting echoes from her flute.

Flower takes over the melody as Jill taps her loop pedal and records sixteen bars of rhythm guitar before picking up the lead again. She moves closer to center stage and starts singing.

"I was walking
I was walking
By the riverside
Listening to the summer wind sing."

Flower plays a smooth, melodious rift, emulating a breeze.

"When my re-ver-ie
Was interrupted
By the voice of the Condo King."

The spotlight shifts to stage right, where a woman wearing a mink stole has appeared. Her meticulously coifed platinum-blond hair is piled high, and in her left arm, she holds a white-and-brown Chihuahua in a diamond-studded collar. She looks at the audience with a painful pout on her ruby-red lips.

"Penelope, Penelope, Penelope Jane
For two million dollars, I can ease your pain."

The woman rocks back and forth with the beat, using her right hand to point toward the river on every half note.

"But Condo King
I'm still feeling blue
Those trees by the river are blocking my view."

Jill boogies across the stage with her fingers moving up and down the neck of her emerald-green Strat. The spotlight follows her until she and the woman are face-to-face, both shimmying to the beat. Jill leans her head back and belts out the next part.

"Don't worry
Don't worry
Penelope Jane."

Jill takes the pitch down an octave and imparts a conspiratorial tone.

"I got a plan straight from the mayor's brain."

JoJo injects nine bars of a throbbing bass rift as the spotlight shifts to the left, where a sinister-looking figure appears from the back in a black cap with red cat ears on top. A long whip is in hand, and he's wearing Dr.

Seuss boxer shorts over a green leotard.

The dancer pulses backward across the stage in a perfect Michael Jackson moonwalk, cracking the whip on the first note of every bar. At the halfway point, JoJo adds a muffled bass explosion to each crack of the whip. The crowd is thrilled, with shrieks and whistles piercing the darkness.

The dancer stops, his back three feet from Jill and blond Penelope Jane, with the whip still cracking to the beat. Jill leans in toward Penelope Jane and sings.

"The trees have to go
If you know what I mean
We'll build a concrete boardwalk to keep your view clean."

Flower's flute howls like a hurricane wind.

"So tell me what you think, Penelope Jane."

Penelope Jane smiles at the audience and blows the dancer a kiss.

"I love the plan
But I don't want to pay
The Condo King and you, must make it go away."

The emerald devil tosses away his whip and breaks into a dance of joy. He works his way back to center stage through an elaborately choreographed routine. Jill and JoJo intertwine melodies with the dancer's rhythmic moves. At center stage, a springboard lets him execute an aerial, full-body twist as Jill's voice comes screaming through the amps.

"We've got a deal.
You'll have your condo with no extra loss
We'll put the citizens in bondage and make them pay the cost
They are there to serve the wealthy
To provide you with a view
It's not about the people
It's just me and you…
And the Condo King."

Jill, Flower, Harpie, and JoJo fly into a wild nine-minute jam that has everyone dancing.

As "The Beast of Bondage" winds down, the crowd's excitement level ramps up. Jill and JoJo confer on center stage before Jill says, "It's all impromptu, folks, but let's let it flow."

JoJo and the band jam for twenty minutes on "Flight of the Android Bees." Jill then pays tribute to Anubis with an extended version of "The Flaming Dogs of Lake Huron." The show ends with Harpie and Flower rolling full tilt on the "William Tell Overture," while Maggie pursues the green devil mayor as he moonwalks around the stage.

The crowd chants, "Pants the mayor, pants the mayor, pants the mayor."

Kidnapped

Coverage of the concert made it onto the evening news. The segment ended with Maggie chasing the green devil mayor. But he held on tight to his underwear.

Midmorning the next day, Melonie dropped by the botanical gardens so she and Thaddeus could walk over to the Hot Rocks Café for a cup of coffee. As they rounded the corner there, Thaddeus saw the housewife and the giant doobie parked in front, sans Rodin's *The Thinker*. Since Søren's filming at Larry's Liquor, the float had been in high demand from local businesses wanting to rent it for events. Funds from the rentals went directly to Maggie's campaign.

Most people had taken to calling the mannequin June. Her 1950s housewife look carried some affinity to the archetypal housewife of the period, June Cleaver, mother to Theodore "Beaver" Cleaver in the sitcom "Leave it to Beaver." But Søren had made some upgrades.

As Thaddeus and Melonie approached Hot Rocks, she gave Thaddeus a sly smile and said, "Watch this." She turned to the mannequin. "Yo, June, what's up?"

A voice emanated from June's immobile, plastic, smiling lips. "Melonie, you're looking good. I see you've got that hunk Thaddeus with you today. I would wink if my eyes weren't painted open. You kids have a great day, and remember to vote for Maggie."

"Will do, June."

The doobie expelled a large puff of fake smoke.

Thaddeus laughed as they entered the café. "Give Søren my compliments."

"Søren put a camera, microphone, and speaker in June's head so whoever's in the booth at his studio—today that's Frita—can remotely talk through the speaker. Frita can see who's on the sidewalk and converse with them. The whole thing is live-streamed on Maggie's campaign website. Talking June has been a big hit. She's brought in close to ten thousand dollars so far."

"Not bad for a mannequin," said Thaddeus.

He ordered his usual Americano, and Melonie settled on a latte before they took seats at a table for two by the front window. Thaddeus had not yet told Melonie how he met and then hired Franky, so he unloaded the entire story over the next fifteen minutes. Melonie listened with a smile and chuckled every once in a while. Thaddeus skipped over the tale of the three thugs and ended with the map he made of buried objects at the abandoned dump.

She sipped her coffee in silence for a full minute after Thaddeus finished. "Little Carl's offer is quite generous. I'll have to contact him. We're going to need a baseline environmental survey before any work begins. That might dampen his enthusiasm. We already have plans drawn up to reclaim the dump site, but a grove of oaks would look nice in the area where Carl wants to landscape."

"I assume an environmental survey requires some degree of subsurface sampling?"

"It does indeed," said Melonie. "In fact, I seem to recall we need to excavate right where he's so nicely drawn the red circle for us." She smiled at Thaddeus. "I'll handle it from here. No need to have suspicions cast on Franky."

·········

(Present)

Thaddeus notices a crowd collecting outside the coffee shop and motions for Melonie to look over her shoulder.

"I wonder what that's about," he says.

Melonie shrugs and drinks the last of her latte. "Let's check it out."

Thaddeus holds the door for her, and as he exits, he immediately spies Pastor Don. The pastor is a fixture around town. He runs the Three Crosses Evangelical Church, with a large campus on the east side of town near the river. Thaddeus thinks Anubis's watery grave may be visible from the church's bell tower, which has attracted a fair bit of controversy since its construction several years ago. It's a three-story carillon-like structure built on the church grounds but free-standing, separated from the other buildings on campus. The ongoing dispute involves the pastor's call to worship: five minutes of vigorous bell-ringing at 6:00 a.m. every Sunday.

Calling Three Crosses a megachurch would be a stretch, but it is still a healthy enterprise with thousands of members and a number of wealthy patrons. Pastor Don is skilled in the religion business and is making a good living.

The church has been sued several times over noise ordinance violations. At one point, the church, being a good neighbor, employed a company that monitored noise levels over a two-month period and demonstrated that the bells registered at 68 decibels in the homes nearest to the church, two decibels below the maximum allowed—Pastor Don is a stickler for the letter of the law.

Some church members believed God originally sent designs for the carillon tower to Pastor Don in a dream—a dream he vigorously described once during a Sunday morning sermon. However, finances and architectural limitations overruled God on the original five-story design. Other, more vicious rumors speculated that the pastor's boyhood job of ringing the Sunday bells at his father's church was more at play than a dreamland message from the Almighty. Regardless of the true reasons for the carillon, the ear-splitting sound of the bells would continue. Pastor Don insisted it was the duty of Christians to rouse unbelievers from their perilous slumber and bring them into the light of the Lord.

The pastor is standing on the sidewalk directly in front of June and appears to be engaged in a philosophical debate. Nine passersby are also engrossed in the discussion. Thaddeus and Melonie join them.

"Well, Pastor, you have referred to my lack of support for Proposition 420 as a position against moral behavior," says June. "I seem to recall that the *Stanford Encyclopedia of Philosophy* provides two definitions of *morality*. One refers to codes of conduct adopted and accepted by groups or individuals. This definition, of course, makes morality subjective, meaning two people could act in different ways, and each could still adhere to their own code of moral conduct. The second definition is a code of conduct that would be accepted by all rational people. Which one are you referring to?"

"Smart mannequin," says the woman next to Melonie.

Melonie whispers to Thaddeus: "I bet you didn't know that Frita has a PhD in philosophy."

He smiles.

"I'm not going to be thrown off by your babble, young woman," says the pastor. "God himself defines morality in his holy written word." Several people clap in response to his defense of morality.

"Sorry, Pastor, I must have missed the verses about cannabis."

"Don't be frivolous with me. God tells us to treat our bodies as his temple. Using drugs is immoral."

A young woman behind Thaddeus comments softly to her partner. "Does he realize he's talking to a mannequin?"

"Hey, wait a minute," says June. "Didn't one of your congregation, Liquor Larry, contribute to that obnoxious bell you ring every Sunday morning? How does liquor jive with morality and the whole body-temple thing?" Frita was party to one of the lawsuits against the church's bell ringing.

This counterpoint draws some claps.

"I don't personally approve of strong drink, but Mr. Oligard runs an honest business."

"Hold on, Pastor Don. Are you saying that the New Amsterdam, just four blocks from here, is not an honest business? It sells legal products to willing customers and fulfills a need in our community. Are you accusing them of illegal activity?"

In the back of his mind, Pastor Don hears his lawyer saying *Don't answer that question*. "I didn't say it was illegal, just immoral, leading our youth into a life of drug addiction."

"Point taken, pastor. But shouldn't we include Larry's Liquor in this category of leading our youth into addiction?"

The doobie lets loose a cloud of smoke and June receives a robust round of applause from the street.

The pastor takes a deep breath to calm himself. "I'm not here for meaningless debate. I'm here as an emissary of God telling you that Proposition 420 is healthy for our community."

No claps ensue.

June gives a "hmmm" as she thinks. "So, just to be clear, you are representing the one and only, the God of Abraham?"

The pastor folds his arms over his chest and narrows his eyes in an apparent stare-off with June. Thaddeus believes this to be an unwise strategy.

"You know I won't blink first in a staring contest," she says.

Vigorous clapping proceeds another puff from the giant doobie.

"Now pastor, I'm literally an empty-headed mannequin. But if I'm not mistaken, our Muslim and Jewish neighbors in North River also worship the God of Abraham. Since all of you folks worship the same God, it appears you should all be receiving the same moral instructions. However, I believe our local Jewish Federation has come out against Proposition 420. This confusing contradiction would make it appear that God is simultaneously for and against the proposition."

"We most certainly do not worship the same as our Jewish and Muslim friends. We worship Christ, the risen Lord. Believe in him, and you will have eternal life."

"If I could move my hand, I would scratch my chin, pastor. I thought you just said you believed in the one and only God, the God of Abraham."

"I do. But for eternal salvation, you also need to believe in Jesus, his son, and the Holy Ghost."

"I see. It's a three-in-one deal. Nonetheless, the same God is speaking to you and the Jewish Federation, yet you have both come to different conclusions on Proposition 420. Assuming God is infallible, it sounds like someone has misunderstood the message. So it could be you. I would say the real message is to vote no since there is a fifty-fifty chance God is in favor of a no vote. Best to hedge your bets on this one."

The clapping is sparse, and Thaddeus believes the shift from philosophy to religious preferences has made people edgy. The street audience has grown since Thaddeus and Melonie first got there, and Pastor Don notices now that multiple video recordings are in progress. He uncomfortably wonders how much of this footage might make it onto the evening news. He addresses June to end the conversation but stumbles midsentence when he contemplates how formally ending a conversation with a mannequin will look on television.

"This is foolishness. I'll be on my way." With that comment, he hurries down the sidewalk.

"Looks like he's headed toward the New Amsterdam," someone says. "I'd be headed there too if I just lost a debate with a plastic mannequin."

June hollers in her loudest mechanical voice: "So long, Pastor Don. Be sure to vote Maggie for Mayor. Thanks for stopping by."

That evening at six, Thaddeus and Melonie relax on her living room couch with two glasses of chardonnay and turn on the news. As they had hoped, one of the amateur vloggers in the crowd had submitted a clip of June and the pastor. Connie Carter is on top of her game, leading the broadcast with "Pastor Don and a mannequin debate the role of religion in modern society."

The vlogger had also taken the time to interview a bystander just before Pastor Don receded from view toward the New Amsterdam. "So, what are your thoughts on the scene we just witnessed?"

The camera focuses on a tattooed man in his early twenties sporting ear hoops and a nose ring. "It's a tough call. Clearly, philosophical debates about religion touch a raw nerve in some people. I suspect the conversation poses some sort of existential threat to their eschatological aspirations. Overall, I would say they both did a reasonable job, but in the end, I think the mannequin had the edge. Her reference to the *Stanford Encyclopedia of Philosophy* was impressive."

"Go, June," says Melonie.

The next day Thaddeus arrives at the botanical gardens at 8:25 a.m. He dismounts his electric scooter, and as he unlocks the front gates, he hears a voice. "Help me, Thaddeus, I'm being kidnapped!"

He twirls around to see the giant doobie float being pulled down

Botanica Drive by a black SUV with tinted windows. June is riding high in the back of the trailer, proudly holding a sign urging onlookers to "Say No to Proposition 420, Vote Maggie."

"Rescue me, somebody, and remember to vote Maggie for Mayor." The voice is slightly muffled by duct tape the kidnapper has placed over June's mouth. The doobie emits three short spurts of smoke followed by three long puffs, then three short puffs again.

Thaddeus recognizes the SOS signal. He mounts his Dorsal Eighteen MAX scooter and enters the chase.

June hollers, "We are passing Botanica and Fifth Street. A kidnapping is in progress! Please call the police. Remember to vote no on the North Bank Development Bond."

Although the doobie blocks Thaddeus's view of the whole license plate, he has gotten close enough to read the last three numbers. But the driver speeds up after realizing a pursuit is in progress. Thaddeus is trying to video record while his scooter bobs up and down over the uneven pavement.

The SUV doesn't slow for a speed bump at Botanica and Seventh, and the doobie trailer goes airborne for a moment. The jolt as it hits the ground causes June's sign-holding arm to fall off and bounce around on the asphalt.

"Heavens to Betsy! What is the world coming to when a simple housewife is kidnapped in broad daylight, all before her morning coffee? And now I don't have another hand to help me. What's going to become of me? Thaddeus, don't let them disappear me like a political dissident. Is Mayor John running a third-world country here in North River? Vote Maggie so this doesn't happen to you."

Thaddeus swerves to avoid June's arm and hopes his phone has picked up her last message. Her voice is getting faint as the SUV's Hemi engine powers it away from the scene of the crime. Thaddeus stops as the SUV rounds a corner two blocks away. He shares his video with Melonie and Officer Jack Trudeau.

Thirty minutes later, on the east side of town, Jolyne notices something odd.

This past Monday marked her third week on the job. She likes working as the receptionist for the Three Crosses Evangelical Church—she is quickly getting the hang of things. And her longtime friend Lisa works there in accounting. They usually eat lunch together and gab about their husbands and kids. The main thing she likes is how friendly the people at the church are. The preacher's wife had been somewhat abrupt when she rushed in ten minutes ago, but she knew Marjorie Wisely was upset about that incident yesterday in front of the coffee shop. Jolyne saw it on yesterday's evening news. She kept her opinion to herself but thought the mannequin had a few good points.

Jolyne stops working on the bulletin for next Sunday's service and stares out the window. There it is again, a wisp of smoke coming from a slightly open window on the ground level of the bell tower. She remembers from her orientation tour of the campus that the bottom floor is used as a utility shed. Sure enough, a steady stream of smoke starts drifting from the building.

"Holy cow, the bell tower is on fire."

Several people in the office rush to the window as Jolyne calls 9-1-1. After she hangs up, Marjorie pops through the office door and asks what the fuss is about.

"It looks like the bell tower is on fire," shouts Sam. He's hard of hearing and believes his voice at a higher volume lets others understand him better.

Marjorie is as still as June for a moment, her eyes wide, but she snaps out of it. "I'm sure it's nothing. I'll go out and have a quick look."

"I've already called the fire department," says Jolyne.

"You did what?" snorts Marjorie before she stomps out of the room, muttering to herself. "That damn mannequin."

Jolyne and her coworkers momentarily stare at one another. A few shrug their shoulders, and everyone goes back to watching the thickening smoke rolling out from the bell tower window.

By the time the fire department arrives, a group of fifteen church staffers has gathered around the base of the bell tower, including Jolyne, who screams at the firefighters: "I think I hear someone inside calling for help."

Everything goes quiet for a moment.

A faint voice is heard: "Please help me. They are trying to do me in! And remember to vote for Maggie."

"Did she say 'remember to vote for Maggie'?" somebody asks.

"I don't know," says another. "But earlier, I could have sworn I heard someone saying to vote no on Proposition 420."

Jolyne hears other voices and puts on her best smile after she turns around: North River News had arrived at the scene just after the fire department, and the cameras are now rolling.

"This is Erika Cool with North River News. We're here on the campus of Three Crosses Evangelical Church, where a fire has broken out in their bell tower. Reports are that someone is trapped inside." Erika directs the camera crew to a better vantage point for capturing the rescue.

Jolyne notices Marjorie standing at a second-floor window in the church, looking dejected.

One fireman takes an ax to the padlock on the utility storage door and flings the double doors wide open. A huge cloud of smoke rolls across the lawn, and a faint voice cries out: "My heroes!"

They drag the megadoobie trailer onto the lawn, where June addresses the crowd. "Thank you all so much. I didn't think I was going to make it through this harrowing ordeal. But in my darkest moments, hope welled up in my hollow chest. I would wave to you, but as you can see, my arm disappeared in an unfortunate mishap somewhere near Botanica and Seventh. But now, thanks to you fine people and these handsome firemen, I am free from my unjust imprisonment and bondage. Speaking of bondage, I urge you to vote against the North Bank Development Bond and vote Maggie Harper for mayor. Would you firemen join me up here?"

Erika Cool smiles at the thought of her footage: armless housewife June flanked by two young firemen, whom she is certain had appeared in last year's Firemen Fundraiser Calendar.

Officer Trudeau and Søren arrive as the fire crew is packing up, and a long, private discussion ensues between them and the pastor's wife. Pastor Don joins in about halfway through. Erika hangs around, filming the meeting from afar. Her hunch is spot-on. They make a deal with Søren—Marjorie issues a public apology for taking the mannequin and float, and Søren declares he won't file charges.

June, duct tape removed from her mouth, pipes up: "All's well that ends well. No hard feelings." Her frozen, plastic smile radiates goodwill and forgiveness.

Marjorie mumbles to herself, "Another place, another time, you plastic bitch."

An Environmental Survey

Carl Jr. was in a funk. He had just gotten off the phone. What he thought would be a smooth win had crumpled into a serious disaster. The curator at the botanical gardens, Thaddeus Barcelona, held up his part of the deal, and the conversation with the river restoration project manager, Melonie, had started well. She seemed genuinely thrilled at the prospect of a donation to install a grove of trees over part of the abandoned dump site. She even commented that his suggested placement of the trees fit with their current draft plans. She was hopeful the landscaping could start within the year.

Then she dropped the bombshell.

What the hell was an environmental baseline study? Why would they waste the money? Why didn't his lawyer tell him about it? Then he recalled he had fired his lawyer. He had not seen the need to consult with him when Franky approached Thaddeus. He only involved him after the fact and was put out when the lawyer said his drawing looked more like a buried treasure map than a real plan. The guy was a loser, so he fired him on the spot and refused to pay his last invoice. He hoped the new lawyer he had just hired could do better.

He pressed the intercom button to speak to his assistant. "Jackie, get Alan Copland on the phone."

Little Carl filled Alan in on his situation without mentioning why he wanted people to avoid digging around at the abandoned dump. Alan was pleased not to know those details.

"Well, Mr. Blankers, state and federal governments require a baseline environmental survey for this sort of project. Besides, it's just good sense for the city to do a survey. It documents the condition of the site before they start any serious work. If future environmental questions arise, the current administration can demonstrate whether the problems are new or preexisting."

"Well, suppose I don't want them to disturb Mother Nature. What can I do to stop it?"

"I am familiar with cases where work was stopped because of archeological concerns—you know, ancient Native American burial sites and such. I suppose there are also regulations for work at sites with historical significance. Give me some time on this. I'll call you back by noon."

Carl Jr.'s phone rang at twelve o'clock sharp.

"What did you find, Alan?"

"The good news is, Mr. Blankers, we have at least a temporary solution. Are you familiar with the name Ezra Babbles?"

"Isn't he the old coot who founded North River? Built it from scratch is what I remember."

"Well, early settlers stole the land from the Native Americans, and then Ezra swindled the factory owners who had started the town. After that, he called himself the city founder."

"Sounds like a smart cookie to me." Carl considered himself a smooth operator and admired people who used the system to cheat others.

Alan let Carl's comment hang in silence for a moment before continuing. "Since Ezra is officially the city's founding father, anything associated with him has historical significance. And it's a fact that the riverside dump site was in operation during Ezra's reign as mayor. Parts of an original building from his time exist just east of the abandoned offices. A third party could file for an injunction against conducting an environmental survey until a full historical survey is completed. If you want to stop the work, I suggest setting up a public-service shell company and filing for an injunction on a historical significance basis."

"I like that, Alan. You're a sharp guy. Let's set up the company and call it Friends of the Earth. The name has a nice ring and sounds like it's into all that liberal environmental mumbo jumbo."

"It's a clever name, Mr. Blankers, but I believe it's already taken. Might I suggest Friends of Ezra? It draws attention to the historical aspect of your case."

"Do it! I'll think of a slogan that describes the good work we're doing."

Alan was dubious about the wisdom of a slogan. "We don't really need a slogan, sir."

"I know we don't need it, but I'm a bit of an expert on how to influence people. And take my word for it—the slogan will help us in the court of public opinion."

Alan sighed softly. "Okay, Mr. Blankers. I'll have the papers ready by the end of the week. Do you want to be listed as the company representative, or would you prefer me to be the representative so your identity is protected?"

Carl Jr. had yet to consider how it would look if he appeared to be the one stopping the work he had agreed to fund. "Perhaps you're onto something here, Alan. You should be the representative."

Carl Jr. hung up and leaned back in his chair. Things were looking up again. "We just get an injunction, and we are home free," he said softly to himself. He tilted his head to the right and caught a glimpse of Jackie's profile. He wondered if his longer-range plan to get her in bed was also swinging in a positive direction.

Brittany, Carl Jr.'s little sister, had spent too many afternoons fretting over what activities her jackass brother was up to. She hired Jackie as an insurance policy several years ago. She was paying her more than Carl Jr. did to be her eyes and ears. Brittany knew that if her dad's business were ever to come under threat, it would be because of Carl Jr.'s stupidity. Now she had a bad feeling she would soon have to make a claim on her insurance policy.

She texted Jackie: *Let's talk.*

Brittany was up to her eyeballs in work related to the North Bank Development Bond, their most significant project on the books. If this deal went south, it wouldn't break them, but still, it would hurt. Two months ago, when the bond initiative finally made it onto the ballot, she thought they were on their way, with clear sailing ahead. But now, with all the fuss the mayor's sister was kicking up, getting the necessary votes at the ballot box was in jeopardy.

She was pissed off at Maggie, but at the same time, she had to admire the woman. Brittany was a born poker player. A quality that made her essential to her dad's real estate business. She was a cold realist who knew when to fold on a bad hand. She could sense the north bank deal was approaching the point where they might have to cut their losses and move on. Mayor John had his strengths, but he was incapable of outshining his sister on the campaign trail. Brittany had hired a private pollster three weeks ago, and thus far, his work on how the bond initiative was sitting with voters was not encouraging. Maggie and her campaign had successfully portrayed the bond as a bid for the average taxpayer to support the ultrawealthy. It wasn't entirely accurate, but she recognized there was enough truth there to sway the public.

She shook her head when her assistant forwarded her a link to the latest news article on the north bank development. It was an opinion piece entitled "Condo King Seeks to Make the People Pay."

"Damn Jill Jammin," she whispered to herself.

Jill's recent concert made the evening news twice, and a special cut of "The Beast of Bondage" went viral on social media and frequently played on several radio stations. Condo Carl as a nickname was bad enough, but now her dad was most often portrayed in the media as the

Condo King, which fed into the public's impression that they were being ripped off. But Brittany knew she would be pissed off about the bond initiative if she were an average taxpayer.

All of this added up to a sickly feeling in the pit of her stomach. Their public support was fading, and Carl Jackass Jr. was about to do something very stupid. She desperately needed to talk to Jackie.

They met at 6:00 p.m. in a booth at the back of the Nasty Cat Bar. It was a well-known LGBTQ+ hangout, and she knew there was zero chance of Carl Jr. or his buddies seeing her and Jackie having a drink there. She ordered a glass of chardonnay, and Jackie asked for a Moscow mule.

Brittany took a sip of wine, sighed, and sat back in her seat. "All right, girl. Tell me what my idiot brother is up to."

Jackie leaned forward and put her elbows on the table. "I think he's really screwed the pooch this time, honey."

Brittany steeled herself for the worst. "Spill the beans. Let me hear it all."

"It started about four weeks ago when Carl had one of his men, Franky, try and blackmail the curator of the botanical gardens. The guy's name is Thaddeus Barcelona, and his girlfriend, Melonie, heads up the north bank restoration project for the city. He was trying to influence Melonie by way of Thaddeus and get her to stop campaigning against the north bank development project. I heard him bragging to his operations manager about how your dad's business would be his soon. You know who Franky is, don't you?"

"Yea, I've met Franky several times."

"Well, you know Franky is a big guy—he also works as a bouncer—but you might not know that inside, he's a softy. Nothing like your brother. No offense."

"None taken. Carl Jr. is a bona fide asshole."

"Well, let me tell you what happened. In the middle of trying to coerce Thaddeus, Franky ended up working for him. The guy offered Franky a job at the botanical gardens. Carmen, his wife, told me Franky loves plants, so taking the job was a no-brainer for him. But everything I've told you so far, namely Carl's attempt to blackmail two city institutions, is the good news."

"Jesus Christ," said Brittany as she took a gulp of chardonnay. "Okay, give me the bad news."

"You aren't going to believe this, honey. Thaddeus turned the tables and convinced Carl to negotiate on something else besides the condos, which he did to save face. Oddly he ended up promising to fund a tree-planting project at the old riverside dump."

Brittany rubbed her forehead like a migraine was coming on. "There is not a philanthropic bone in that twit's body. He's up to something."

"I only got a glimpse of it, Brittany, but Carl made a map of the dump and drew a red circle around the area where he wanted the trees planted. You know, he fired his attorney last week when the guy told him the drawing looked like a buried treasure map."

"I didn't know. Send me the name of his new attorney when you get a chance."

"There's something buried at that old, abandoned dump, and Carl doesn't want whatever it is dug up. He thought he had won when Melonie contacted him and sweet-talked him about his generous offer. Then she dropped the bomb that they'd need a baseline environmental survey before any planting started. That blew his tiny mind, and now he and the new lawyer are concocting some scheme to get an injunction to stop it. Carl doesn't understand the difference between a permanent injunction and a preliminary injunction. It hasn't hit him yet that he's simply delaying the problem, not solving it."

Brittany downed the remaining half glass of wine and held her hand up to the server to bring another round. "Against my better judgment, I suppose I'll have to bail my brother out. Daddy wouldn't forgive me if I let him drown in his own incompetence. I need you to do me a favor and dig back into Carl's records to the period just after the dump closed. See if anything jumps out at you."

"Sure thing, honey." Jackie slid her hand over Brittany's. "Do you need any company tonight?" Jackie was dressed to kill in her usual office wear that kept Little Carl salivating and her sitting outside his office. Brittany wasn't currently in a relationship, and she and Jackie had dated years ago. Technically, Jackie was her employee, but the freelance nature of the contract offered some flexibility.

Brittany eyed her up and down with a smile. "How could I say no."

The next day Brittany started on her new plan. Her assistant arranged a telephone call with Melonie at noon. After doing some research, Brittany discovered she and Melonie had been high school classmates, but a year apart. She didn't remember Melonie.

The phone rang twice before Melonie picked up.

"Melonie, this is Brittany Blankers. I appreciate you taking some time to talk with me today."

"Sure, Brittany, no problem. It's been a while since high school. You've done well for yourself." Melonie remembered.

"It's a double-edged sword to work for your dad. But he's taught me a lot, and I carry my own weight. You've done well too. The city is lucky to have you, even though we're at odds with each other on the north bank development. I suppose it's no secret that I'm calling you about that project. You're running a good campaign for Maggie, winning over the voters by opposing the bond. This presents me with some tough decisions. I'm calling because I'd like to get a better understanding of your vision for the entire riverbank restoration—not just the area affected by the bond and the condo development. I want to understand the whole picture."

"It's difficult to describe the restoration over the phone. Could you drop by my office for an hour this afternoon? I can walk you through it."

The women met and spent over two hours discussing the details of the restoration plan. Even though it was a barrier to her real estate aspirations, Brittany was impressed with Melonie's vision for the riverside. Brittany also garnered some important information: the plot of land occupied by the dump was an add-on to the original architectural design.

Melonie casually mentioned Carl Jr.'s interest in restoring the dump. She was fishing, but Brittany didn't take the bait.

"I'm never fully sure what's going on in Little Carl's brain," said Brittany. "But let me give you some advice. He's mercurial—he runs hot on something one day and cold on it the next. It's always best to get any agreements with him in writing."

By the time their session ended, Brittany had a workable plan in the back of her mind. She just needed some information from Jackie before approaching her dad.

She and Jackie shared drinks again that evening at the Nasty Cat. Jackie had hit pay dirt while searching through Carl Jr.'s company files.

"I think I know what that slippery little turd is up to, Brittany. And if I'm right, he's worked his way into a real mess this time."

Brittany sighed and motioned for Jackie to continue.

"At the same time the dump closed, Carl signed a contract with Nuool Industrial. I don't know much about what they produce, but they end up with an extremely toxic byproduct. This sludge needs specialized processing at a licensed facility. Carl's contract was to collect and dispose of twenty-seven barrels of it."

Brittany held up her hand to pause Jackie. "Let me guess. He buried the barrels at the dump right after it closed down, but when there was still cleanup traffic. Then he charged Nuool the full cost of disposal."

Jackie pushed a xeroxed copy of a signed receipt from the disposal facility for twenty-seven barrels of waste. Brittany examined the signature. There was no question about it being her brother's handwriting.

"People go to prison for this type of shit," said Jackie. "If the restoration project digs up those barrels, your brother is going to jail. The barrels will be traced to Nuool, and they'll produce the receipt from none other than Carl Jr. Listen, you have to step in and do something. I deliberately didn't take pictures of any of this paperwork—evidence will certainly not end up on my phone. I only copied the one receipt."

"You're clean, Jackie. Don't dig through any more files. Just continue to keep your ears open for me. I'm going to have a conversation with my idiot brother soon."

Philosopher's Stone

Cranstone had kept a low profile during the campaign. He occasionally appeared with Maggie at her rallies, but thus far, he had declined all requests by North River News to interview him. He knew that his tendency to wander off into the dusty, cobwebbed corners of philosophy would not help Maggie's campaign if seen on the evening news.

Lately, though, he had taken his mind off the campaign by preparing for his opening address at the Philosopher's Stone Conference. This year marked the tenth anniversary of the symposium. Cranstone had presented papers at nine of them and served on the organizing committee for several years. At the past three meetings, he had presented papers on his favorite topic, delusional humanism. This year, he intended to promote more interest in his arcane branch of modern philosophy.

His book, *Dysfunction in Modern Society and Its Roots in Delusional Humanism* was published just a month ago. Sales were low thus far, meaning none, and Cranstone reasoned that this conference was his chance to bring his theories and his book into the limelight. While the book devoted a chapter to the now disgraced ex-president Daniel Rump, Cranstone was veering away from mentioning him—too many news cycles had spun that story, and the fact that the old guy was locked up in some posh prison for rich criminals made a Rump-themed talk seem pitiful.

His book spent more time on climate change than Rump, so he focused his opening address on the widespread denial of climate change in the face of increasing climate disasters. He had narrowed the talk down to an in-depth treatment of the Florida insurance conundrum. The scientific facts in the Florida quandary were very clear. Global sea levels were rising from melting ice caps and the thermal expansion of ocean water. Florida, a state at basically zero feet of elevation above sea level, was not rising. When viewed this way, even the simplest of minds could grasp that the entire state was a flood disaster waiting to happen.

The problem with living in a hurricane-prone flood zone is that damage to your home is inevitable. It's not a matter of *if* you will experience flooding; it's only a matter of *when*. Breathtakingly strong winds and monster storm surges could lift your home from its foundation in minutes and deposit it in your neighbor's yard. These risks were not hypothetical. They occurred in real-time each year during hurricane season, and they provided a business opportunity for insurance companies.

Over time, many of these Florida insurance operations went bankrupt by assuming past damages were a reliable indicator of future damages. They failed to understand the significance of the term *change* in *climate change*.

As private companies were reluctant to lose more money in the Florida insurance market, the state politicians panicked and agreed to use taxpayer dollars to prop up insurance shortfalls. Banks were typically reticent to lend mortgage funds to homeowners who might lose everything during the next hurricane season. They wanted proof that their investment was insured.

With much of the state's economy depending on real estate, politicians were desperate to perpetuate the myth that Florida was a tropical paradise. Many decades of work had gone into the illusion that a warm oceanside utopia could be had by anyone. But without insurance, the mortgage market might dry up, and without lenders, homeowners would have to take their dreams elsewhere.

The answer was to pretend the problem didn't exist. The message currently being delivered didn't focus on the fact that Florida was slowly sinking below the waves like the lost continent of Atlantis. No, the problem was recast to emphasize how gutless, risk-averse insurance companies were shirking their responsibility to prop up Florida's housing market.

Common sense would inform most people that insurance only works when lots of people pay into the system and only a few people suffer damages and make claims. But the system breaks down when everyone has the same high risk of disaster. This basic logic escaped the state legislature and Governor Don Rantos. The powers that be said taxpayers should make mandatory payments into a state disaster and reinsurance program to keep the real estate business rolling. After all, there were a handful of wealthy campaign donors who depended on an ever-rising real estate market. What could possibly go wrong?

In retrospect, many people were beginning to realize that the entire state couldn't insure itself out of climate change. Annual tax assessments to support the system were rising, and a string of disasters kept Florida's disaster and reinsurance funds perpetually in the red. Unfortunately, those people who saw the faulty logic in the state's insurance system were not the ones living in Florida or running its government. So, twenty-two million Floridians lived under the mass delusion that climate change, rising seas, and more frequent killer storms were not the problem; it was the broken insurance market. It's human nature to avoid existential dilemmas, which made the Florida insurance catastrophe a good study of delusional humanism, according to Cranstone.

Cranstone found his preparatory research interesting. He raised his eyebrows when he discovered that about forty percent of sea level rise since the 1950s was attributable to expanding oceans, not melting ice. Water, like most substances, expands as it warms. Global warming ensured the oceans would rise from thermal expansion alone. Melting ice was just a bonus.

Then there was the issue that a warmer climate, leading to warmer oceans, raised sea level temperatures in the tropics. Tropical storms, including hurricanes, derive their energy from warm ocean water; the hotter the water, the greater the frequency of intense hurricanes. Cranstone saw an intrinsic beauty in the cause-and-effect relationships between climate change and the demise of Florida. It was terribly inconvenient for those living there, but the fact that the Florida real estate market kept on growing in the face of irreversible climate change threats only added to Cranstone's enthusiasm for using climate change denial as a prime example of delusional humanism. He smiled to himself as he pieced together his opening address.

As Cranstone prepared, another person was applying to attend the conference. Since Cranstone was not on this year's organizing committee, he didn't know that, for the first time in a decade, a press pass had been requested. The organizing committee was thrilled when Erika Cool of North River News applied for a pass to cover the opening day at the conference. They would have been disappointed to know that her primary objective was an interview with Cranstone. The Harper versus Harper mayoral race was a hot topic, and Erika had garnered some state-wide recognition for her campaign coverage thus far.

The race between Maggie and her brother was close. Maggie had been wildly successful in swinging the voters her way on two initiatives: all polls so far indicated Proposition 420 and the North Bank Development Bond were going down in flames. But Mayor John had pulled out older news footage of Maggie's Free the Bees campaign to promote the image of his older sister as a well-meaning but eccentric geriatric. And he used a picture of Maggie hobbling with a walker after she suffered an ankle injury in a half marathon run two years ago. The political ad read; *Let's give our elderly the rest they deserve. Reelect John Harper to retain a younger generation of leadership.* The most recent polls placed them in a dead heat.

On the first day of the conference, academic and amateur philosophers gathered at the community college's fine arts building for the opening ceremonies. Thaddeus was in the front lobby with the crowd. He didn't have any burning interest in philosophy beyond his life equation, but he wanted to support Cranstone, and he liked hearing some of the wild and wacky talks. He was surprised to see Søren on the other side of the room, in deep discussion with a slender, attractive woman. Thaddeus, reading their body language, surmised their conversation was much more social in nature than professional.

He already had a mug of Americano from Hot Rocks, but he stopped by the breakfast table and grabbed a chocolate croissant on his way to Søren.

"Thaddeus, good to see you. This is an old acquaintance of mine, Cassie. Cassie, meet Thaddeus, Melonie's partner."

Thaddeus was glad to see he had graduated from boyfriend to partner. It seemed more permanent. He could feel his life equation shifting. "What brings you here today, Søren?"

"My father's predilection toward philosophy was ingrained in me at an early age, and fortunately or unfortunately, philosophical discussions are my muse to spark artistic inspiration."

Thaddeus wasn't quite sure what to say and was glad when Cassie stepped in.

"Søren, I thought you said I was your muse when you painted a nude of me last year."

Søren leaned over a gave her hand a squeeze. "An artist can have more than one muse, my dear woman."

The lights in the foyer flickered, indicating the opening ceremony would start in a few minutes. Søren looked over his shoulder at the doors as people started streaming in. "Come sit with us, Thaddeus. I understand you and Cranstone are close acquaintances."

"I've known the Professor for many years, but I'll be the first to admit I don't really understand him."

"Have you read his latest book?" asked Cassie.

Thaddeus shook his head in the negative.

"I bought it two days ago and finished it last night," she continued. "I found it to be a damning critique of groupthink. He makes some good points about the delusional nature of our relationships with the world around us. But, after all, existentialism says that reality is subjective at best. Everyone sees the same event from a slightly different perspective, so no two people share the exact same version of reality."

Thaddeus nodded. "Reality is subjective, and the human psyche easily slips into abject self-deception."

Søren remarked in an absent-minded tone, "*Abject self-deception.* I can visualize it, and all art is first found in the mind of the artist."

Thaddeus wondered what artistic creation that thought might lead to.

....

(Present)

The three take their seats. After eighteen minutes of effusive comments on the importance of the Philosopher's Stone Conference, Cranstone is introduced. He makes his way onto the stage, giving the impression of a man who might possibly be lost and has accidentally stumbled upon an audience. Thaddeus is familiar with this entrance, having previously seen Cranstone speak several times.

Thaddeus glances at the front row and spies Erika Cool. He quickly looks behind himself and sees the North River News camera rolling. "This can't be good," he whispers to Søren while pointing at the back of the theater.

Søren madly taps on his phone, sending a note to Melonie.

Cranstone is not a natural-born speaker, but he has developed techniques to give a good show. One of them is to look at the audience as if he is scanning their faces while he talks. In reality, they are all just a blur. He never focuses on a single person, as this makes him lose concentration and stumble. This is the reason he doesn't recognize Erika Cool, even though he looks directly at her several times. As he finishes his opening address, a gentle and polite round of applause fills the lecture hall.

The master of ceremonies steps up to the microphone and asks if there are any questions. After letting several academics seek clarification on some of the finer points in Cranstone's presentation, he motions for Erika Cool to ask the next question. The MC, desperate for media coverage of the conference, is thrilled that North River News is present and envisions possible state-wide or national recognition of the conference.

One of the ushers helping with the Q&A hands Erika a mic. "Professor Fletcher, I'm Erika Cool with North River News. We're excited to be covering the Philosopher's Stone Conference. I just read your book, and I'm interested to know if your theories of delusional humanism are playing a role in the current mayoral election."

Cranstone smiles when he hears that at least one copy of his book has sold. He feels a bit confident after successfully delivering his opening address, and he spies the camera crew. Thaddeus is not as enthused and recalls several past incidents when the Professor turned the tide against himself by using hypotheticals. He hopes against all hope the Professor will stick with the facts and reality.

"Excellent question, Ms. Cool, and I appreciate your interest in these proceedings. Delusion is part of the human psyche, and we all are victims of occasional lapses to one degree or another. By and large, this election has rested on the strengths and weaknesses of two main issues: Proposition 420 and the North Bank Development Bond. The candidates—my dear wife and her brother—have debated on these issues, generally based on the facts but including, of course, the usual political hyperbole. But hypothetically speaking, things could always take a turn for the worst."

"Don't go there, Professor," Thaddeus says in a low tone that only Søren hears. Thaddeus's phone vibrates with a text as Erika lifts her microphone for a follow-up. Melonie's frantic reply to Søren's message, which has included Thaddeus, reads, *How bad is it?*

"Perhaps you could give us an example of how manic social delusion could unfold in this election."

Cranstone's face lights up at Erika's mention of one of his key concepts. Thaddeus recognizes the look and responds to Melonie: *The ship is sinking,* followed by a sad-face emoji.

"I would be delighted to provide a hypothetical example. Several times your news coverage has included the campaign advertising mannequin, who is known as June, a reference to June Cleaver."

Søren, being a thoughtful artist and the campaign media director, has an apocalyptic vision and shakes his head back and forth, mouthing "No."

Cranstone continues, "Now, everyone realizes that neither June the mannequin nor June the TV character represent a real person. If, however, a widespread movement broke out to elect June as mayor, we would indeed be seeing a case where individual people recognize reality, but as a group, they are suffering from a mass social delusion. Such a break from reality is more frequent than you might expect."

Thaddeus is live broadcasting the conversation to Melonie. She texts him nine flame emoji.

"Well, fortunately, Dr. Fletcher, June Cleaver is not on the ballot."

"No, the unfortunate souls who want to vote for her will have to do so as a write-in candidate."

Thaddeus has his speaker on mute, but he still faintly hears Melonie's scream floating across the broadband ether. Søren vacates his seat and scurries toward the exit doors with Cassie in tow. Cranstone has blissfully moved on to the next question like a wrecking ball gracefully arcing upward after taking out a VW Beetle at the low point of its trajectory.

That evening, Cranstone sits in his living room with Maggie and Melonie as the news starts.

"This is Connie Carter with North River News. In an unexpected statement today, Professor Cranstone Fletcher, husband of mayoral candidate Maggie Harper, raised the possibility of a third candidate in the race for mayor, the advertising mannequin June Cleaver." They cut to Erika's comment about June not being on the ballot and then to Cranstone's response.

He considers that his response was not as well-worded and witty as he imagined at the time. Frigid stares from both Maggie and Melonie confirm his suspicions. Cranstone picks up the bong on the side table next to him and takes a hit. He gets up and disappears into his study, smoke rippling behind him.

"C'est la vie," he says to an empty room. "Such is the life of a philosopher."

Cranstone searches his bookshelves for Dante's "Inferno" and collapses into his desk chair to determine which of the nine circles of hell he is in. He first considers the sixth circle, heresy, where unfortunate souls are trapped in flaming tombs. He toys with the idea of the ninth circle, where betrayers of special relationships are frozen in a lake of ice. But he finally settles on the more benign first circle, limbo, since it is reserved for virtuous pagans.

Shifting Ground

Melonie shook her head as she sifted through the latest polling results. Two weeks had passed since Cranstone's unintentional endorsement of June as a candidate for mayor. Last week a 3 percent uptick in voters for June Cleaver accompanied a 2 percent drop in support for Maggie. This week was worse. A full 9 percent supported June.

On her way home from work two nights ago, she passed the doobie mobile parked in front of the Hot Rocks Café again. June was pitching Maggie for Mayor, but several women on the street were shouting, "No, June. We want you!"

June modestly declined. "You know I love all of my fans. But really, I'm a mannequin. Vote for Maggie, and maybe she will make me her special assistant."

Not a chance in hell thought Melonie. She made a mental note to talk to Søren. Maggie's campaign was spiraling out of control, and June was like a Ferris wheel broken loose from its frame, crashing through the circus grounds.

"No, June. It can't be anyone else. You are the one," hollered a woman on roller skates, who appeared to be preparing for a Mardi Gras parade with vibrant purple, green, and gold hair.

"Yes," shouted a newcomer. "June is the chosen one."

Melonie and Søren had stopped renting out the doobie mobile, but when they tried to cancel the appearances already booked, they were met with stiff resistance. June was evidently good for business, and they had signed contracts. One customer had questioned whether they were attempting to manipulate the election by silencing one of the candidates. It was a lose-lose situation for the campaign.

Mayor John had stretched his lead by two percentage points. Apparently, his supporters were less enthusiastic about a plastic mannequin for mayor than Maggie's. With election day not far away, Melonie needed some way to reverse the downhill slide.

While she contemplated her options, Jessie's face appeared in the office doorway with a frown. "I know you aren't having a good day, and I'm afraid this will make it worse. We were slapped with a temporary injunction this morning, halting any environmental survey work on the old city dump site."

Melonie motioned for her assistant to drop her paperwork on the desk, and "Thanks" was her only reply.

Jessie retreated from Melonie's office.

Melonie dragged the documents across the desk and started reading. As she worked her way through the injunction, she quickly identified a group called Friends of Ezra as the source of this nonsense. She shuffled through the papers and located their contact information. Then her eyes zoomed to the italics at the base of the page, part of the organization's messaging: Friends of Ezra—Saving Historically Interesting Trash.

"Carl Jr. has to be behind this," she remarked to no one. "Who else is going to let their company be known as FOE SHIT? That slimy toad is hiding something and wants to wiggle out of his predicament."

She hollered for Jessie and waited for her to stick her head through the office door. "Legal knows about this, I assume?"

"They're on the case, Melonie. Also, since you have a lot on your plate right now, I was intercepting your messages when Brittany Blankers rang. She wants to meet with you."

Melonie raised her eyebrows. For reasons unknown, her gut instincts were seeing some sunshine at the end of a bleak morning. "Thanks, I'll call her back."

Brittany was cagey and wanted to avoid meeting in the city offices, so they agreed to a lunchtime meeting at Hot Rocks. Unfortunately for Melonie, her plastic nemesis was on contract there all week.

....

(Present)

Melonie approaches Hot Rocks and immediately spots the A-frame sidewalk sign in front of the doobie mobile. White letters on a dark blue background highlight the words *June for Mayor*. Melonie sighs and assumes the same message is on the other side of it. She stops in front of June and stares. After a moment, the giant doobie emits a puff of smoke.

"Sorry, Melonie. The more I tell them to vote for Maggie, the more they want to vote for me. If my smile wasn't permanently fixed on my face, I would be frowning with you."

"Just do your best to convince them a mannequin cannot serve as mayor and hope rational thinking will prevail."

She folds up the A-frame, carries it into the café, and hands it to Carol, who is wise enough to just take it and slip it behind the counter. The only available table is at the window, where she has a front-row view of June. Melonie faintly hears several people speaking outside.

"June, tell us who took the sign. We know you saw it," someone says.

"I'm not the kind of girl to kiss and tell. Now really, you need to be voting for Maggie."

"We're looking for a change, new blood. Someone with a vision," shouts a man wearing a North River Community College hoodie.

"I'm plastic. I don't have blood, and I don't have visions. Vote for Maggie. I'm telling you, it's the only way to make a change."

"You're real enough for me, June Cleaver," he replies. "I've been a fan ever since you were rescued from the kidnapping. Using the doobie to send SOS smoke signals was a stroke of genius. You have what it takes."

June doesn't reply but sends out a puff of smoke.

Brittany walks through the door and strolls over to Melonie's table. "Thanks for taking the time to meet with me."

"No problem. I already ordered a sandwich but asked them to hold off until you got here."

Brittany heads to the counter as Melonie sips her latte, contemplating how to get Maggie back in the game. The options are limited. June is sucking up votes on an uncontrolled upward trajectory.

As Brittany settles into the seat across from Melonie, she glances at the small crowd. "Søren's creation is quite the hit."

"Are you two acquainted?"

"No. But I own several of his paintings."

"I have one that Thaddeus bought me recently. I really like it."

"It isn't the one with the dirt road and farmhouse, is it?"

"Yes, Road to Buddha's Farm. It was on display here for a while."

Brittany inhales deeply and lets out a breath. "I had been admiring it for several weeks, and when I finally convinced myself to buy it, it was too late. Your partner has good taste."

Brittany looks again at the crowd and decides now is the time to play her hand. "I have a proposition I want to discuss with you. You've run a slick campaign up until the June Cleaver debacle. But even with that setback, you've eviscerated the north bank development project. My dad is beside himself, but I'm a practical businesswoman. I'm not happy about the bond initiative failing, but we don't always get what we want. I'm certainly not going to chase a lost cause. What if we pull out of the deal and, as a gesture of goodwill, buy the land the old city dump is on and build a historic park?"

Melonie takes a long pause. "You aren't the only one suddenly interested in the historical significance of that land." She hands Brittany a copy of the injunction papers.

While Brittany scans the documents, Melonie tunes back into the faint sidewalk conversation. The crowd has thinned to three people. "Yes, I understand that the mannequins in that movie developed consciousness. But that's not going to happen to me, so vote for Maggie."

"You never know, babe." It's the student with the hoodie. "Like, what if you got struck by lightning, and it induced some quantum weirdness? Maybe you would become entangled with a human brain."

"First of all, don't call me babe. I'm old enough to be your mother." Hoodie Boy looks at his feet and shuffles a bit. "Secondly, that is not how quantum entanglement works. The first thing to know about the quantum world is that particles like electrons or photons don't exist at any specific location. It's not like Earth orbiting the sun. The location of a photon can only be described by a probability wave function. This means that we don't know where the photon is; we just know the probability that it could be at specific locations. So when two super fast-moving particles smack into each other, that interaction can cause them to become entangled, meaning that the state of one particle is linked to the state of the other particle. If the state of one changes, then the state of the other changes instantly. Now let me make this clear: no human brains traveling close to the speed of light are going to smack into me, so I am definitely not going to become entangled with a human brain. Vote for a real human brain. Vote for Maggie."

Hoodie Boy is momentarily stunned before he speaks. "You are one frigging smart mannequin. I am definitely voting for you."

June remains silent but emits a series of smoke puffs, which Melonie imagines translate to "Shit, I tried."

Brittany has missed the sidewalk conversation and pushes the papers back to Melonie's side of the table. "FOE SHIT? What kind of moron lets that be the acronym for their organization? I honestly didn't know about the injunction. Not necessarily related to this document, I will say that my brother's hormone-riddled brain fails daily to understand the magnitude of his incompetence. But despite the tidal wave of asinine ideas that come out of my brother's mouth, he is still family. And I hope you'll understand if I don't discuss this document in more detail."

Melonie can play poker almost as well as Brittany. "I need a public announcement."

Brittany is taken aback. "What?"

"A public announcement that you're pulling out of the north bank development deal."

Brittany is looking Melonie in the eye, but in her head, she is smacking Carl Jr. on his nose with a rolled newspaper screaming, "Bad dog! Bad dog!"

"Done."

"Let me be clear, Brittany. I can't guarantee the city will sell you the land. Assuming they can, I will recommend that you should have responsibility for cleaning it up—and I mean scrubbing it spotless aboveground and below. Final third-party verification will be necessary before any historical park is built."

"I understand."

The two women shake hands, and Brittany leaves. Shortly after, Melonie exits the café, climbs onto the doobie mobile, and whispers into June's plastic ear.

Franky arrives at the botanical gardens the next morning and makes finding Thaddeus his first order of business.

Thaddeus is sipping a freshly brewed coffee in greenhouse 9, contemplating his new French press. It's double-screened to provide maximum filtering, but he can still taste some small granules. He walks to his coffee station on the other side of the greenhouse and selects a coarser setting on his grinder. The brewing process is a lot like his life equation, where adjustments in one area ultimately require readjusting in another to achieve unity. In this case, the larger granules have less total surface area, so more beans must be ground. He leaves a note for himself to use five scoops of beans tomorrow.

Franky's arrival diverts his attention, and Thaddeus gives him a wave as he enters the greenhouse.

Franky is only halfway down the main aisle when he shouts, "Congratulations, I just heard the good news—the condo deal is dead. Now I can coordinate our riverbank garden with Melonie's team."

This announcement is news to Thaddeus. "Where did you hear that?"

"June told me when I stopped at Hot Rocks for a morning cup."

"June?"

"Yeah, she got an anonymous tip."

Thaddeus looks at his schedule for the day. His morning is blank, so he heads out. When he arrives at the café, he gets close to the doobie mobile and scans the street to ensure he is alone. He speaks in a low voice. "June, is it true you're telling people the development deal is dead?"

"They aren't just rumors, Thaddeus. It's true."

"Does Melonie know about this?"

"Yes. She and Brittany Blankers cut a deal yesterday."

Thaddeus considers this. "Does she know that you know are spreading the word?"

She responds in a voice he can barely hear: "Not exactly."

Before Thaddeus can digest the intel, he sees Erika Cool's face in the passenger window of a news van as it passes him and pulls over to the curb. Thaddeus is on the move and rounding the corner when Erika cries out, "Wait, Thaddeus. I have a question for you."

He pauses long enough to holler back, "Sorry, Erika, we have an emergency at the gardens. I have to run."

He hears Erika in the distance as he breaks into a slow run. "What kind of emergency? Should the film crew and I drop by?"

That evening, Melonie and Thaddeus experience low-level trepidation as she switches on the television.

"This is Connie Carter with North River News. It seems that our city's favorite mannequin, June Cleaver, has been instrumental in brokering a deal with Carl Blankers Sr., the Condo King, on the north bank development."

Melonie lurches forward, choking on her wine.

Thaddeus pats her on the back. "Steady on."

"Our viewers will recall that several weeks ago, June thwarted a kidnapping by sending smoke signals from the bell tower at Three Crosses Evangelical Church. No charges were filed against the alleged kidnapper, Marjorie Wisely, wife of the church's pastor, Don Wisely. Let's go to Erika Cool, who interviewed June this morning."

"This is Erika Cool coming to you from outside the Hot Rocks Café. We're here with June." The camera cuts to June's stoic face. "Tell me, have you recovered from your recent kidnapping nightmare?"

"Oh, Erika, I prefer to consider it a misunderstanding. No harm was done."

"No harm, June? You lost your right arm."

"Nothing that a few new bolts and some superglue couldn't solve, and I'm right as rain now. I'm sure Mrs. Wisely has moved on too. All of us have an occasional bad-hair day. Well, except for me, since I just have a wig glued onto my head."

On the east side of town, Pastor Don steals a look at his wife as they watch the news. He is concerned by her clenched teeth, narrowed eyes, and white knuckles as she leans forward and grips the arms of the white Victorian chair next to his.

"How do you feel about the groundswell of support for your mayoral campaign?" Asks Erica. "You're now polling at 9 percent."

"I love my fans, Erika, and I'm sure they're just poking fun at the pollsters. Even though I can't vote, I am firmly supporting Maggie for mayor. Everyone knows I wouldn't even be able to manage a ribbon-cutting ceremony since my opposable thumbs are nonfunctional."

The camera switches back to Erika. "Yet somehow, June, you seem to have influenced the recent announcement by Blankers Real Estate that they are withdrawing from the north bank development project, leaving Mayor John Harper high and dry on his ballot initiative for the bond. How did you do it?"

The giant doobie emits a puff of smoke as the camera pans back to June. "Really, Erika, you give me too much credit. I simply had a few conversations with people about Maggie Harper's vision for the ecological restoration of our beautiful riverbanks. Maggie has a meaningful long-term plan for the future of North River. I urge all your viewers to vote for Maggie. Don't waste a vote on me."

The action switches back to Connie. "Well, there we have it. Reluctant write-in candidate June Cleaver is already cutting deals."

Defenestration

Events leading up to election day were tumultuous at best. June's contracts ended nine days before the election, and Søren, Melonie, and Maggie put her into storage. Her new home was in a garage attached to Søren's art studio. The management team's decision was based on the *out of sight, out of mind* concept, which turned out to be wrong in this case. Less than twenty-four hours after her disappearance, rumors and speculation took hold on social media platforms. The leading theory was she was being held prisoner by the North River Secret Police, something the police chief and Mayor John vehemently denied. Protesters were not deterred by the fact that North River had no secret police. Instead, they insisted there was no way to know since, by definition, this off-the-books operation was secret.

Maggie's campaign felt compelled to bring June back, minus the doobie mobile. The Hot Rocks Café agreed to let her stand in their front window for the duration of the campaign. Søren, taking no chances that she might be able to converse with her admirers, removed all the microphones and speakers but left her main camera in place. Silent June continued to wear her blue-and-white plaid dress and hold a *Vote for Maggie* sign. Despite Søren's precautions, June was polling at close to 30 percent the week before election day.

Crowds gathered daily outside Hot Rocks Café, urging passersby to vote for June. Hoodie Boy from North River Community College was June's self-proclaimed campaign manager. Erika Cool had covered him one evening when he explained that write-in candidate June Cleaver had taken a vow of silence until the election.

The only good news from Melonie's standpoint was that the collapse of the north bank development deal had shifted Maggie one percentage point above Mayor John in the polls.

Cranstone's interest in the election ticked up a few notches as these events unfolded. On the surface, he frowned along with Maggie when the subject of June's voter appeal came up. But inside, he was hopping with joy. June's meteoric rise in the poles had attracted the national press. They ran a number of Erika Cool's pieces, including her questions from the Philosopher's Stone Conference. His book sales spiked, and his publisher initiated a new run to satisfy the demand. Cranstone was convinced his big break had arrived, and he wasn't going to waste the opportunity. He was on the ground each day, hanging with the *Vote for June* crowd and conducting as many interviews as possible. Initially, his lead question was simple: *Why are you voting for June?* The compendium of answers provided a goldmine of information for a detailed case study of delusional humanism:

> *"June is the bomb. That's why I'm voting for her."*
>
> *"Yes, I know she's just a mannequin, but her charisma is overwhelming."*
>
> *"I wish she hadn't taken her vow of silence. I would love to know what she's thinking right now. I'm voting so I can hear her acceptance speech at the swearing-in ceremony."*
>
> *"She has got to be the smartest mannequin alive. That alone qualifies her for mayor."*

After several days, he progressed to a more forward-looking question: *What makes June a good leader?*

> *"She knows when to be quiet."*
>
> *"Her vision for the future is undeniably brilliant. Creating a city in ecological balance with nature is a beautiful long-term vision. The fact that she single-handedly destroyed the north bank condo development says it all."*
>
> *"She is tough on law and order, and she's smart. Even when she was kidnapped, she kept a level head and resolved the conflict without resorting to violence."*
>
> *"Politicians talk a lot and do nothing. The worse that can happen with June is she says nothing and does nothing, which would be an improvement over what we currently have."*

Cranstone envisioned how documenting this election could catapult his theory into the limelight. He started writing an update to his Wikipedia page, describing himself as the father of the modern delusional humanism movement.

Cranstone was probably the most engaged person in North River with regard to the election. He did want Maggie to win, of course, but he couldn't help being excited at the prospect of June winning. Melonie was less enthusiastic about June's popularity and recently had several dreams where June was floating on the river atop a burning funeral pyre. The last week of the election was packed with action. The two registered candidates made appearances all around town as June silently watched her voter base grow.

Maggie called out her brother's loss of the north bank development deal as a clear sign he was inept. He countered by standing firm on his record. Some people considered this a mistake; beyond getting elected, there was little he had in the way of concrete accomplishments.

Thaddeus kept his distance from the political fray and maintained heightened vigilance for signs of Erika Cool. He most definitely did not want to be interviewed. She knew he was a major donor to Maggie's campaign and was keen to talk about it. His ringtone for Erika was a clip from "The Flaming Dogs of Lake Huron."

It was clear on election day that voter turnout was at an all-time high. If nothing else, the vigorous campaigning of the past several months had gotten voters off their warm comfy couches and into the polling stations. By nine o'clock that evening, the polls were closed, and vote counting was well underway. As the precincts reported, three things became apparent. Proposition 420 was heavily trending toward a *No* vote, the North Bank Development Bond Issue resembled the Hindenburg disaster, and the mayor's race was a nail-biter. Maggie, Mayor John, and June were all within one percent of each other.

At eleven thirty that night, with ninety-nine percent of the vote counted, North River News called the election. June led with thirty-four percent, followed by Maggie with just above thirty-three and Mayor John at slightly under thirty-three.

Erika Cool provided live coverage of the party outside the Hot Rocks Café. June was smiling because she had no choice, and several people chanted, "Speech, speech." The cameras zoomed in on Hoodie Boy as Erika asked him how he felt.

"I'm ecstatic that the good people of North River stood behind the right candidate. It's a great country where a former lingerie model can become mayor. June's humble beginnings on the fifth floor of Porter's Department Store taught her the value of hard work and perseverance. She's no quitter. She ran a good, clean race and won. Mayor-elect June Cleaver has decided to extend her vow of silence until the swearing-in ceremony."

On the east side of town, Pastor Don woke up after his front door slammed shut. He thought it was his son coming home and went back to sleep. Marjorie Wisely, dressed in black with her blond hair tucked neatly under a black stocking cap, moved like a ninja across the driveway. She checked over her shoulder several times and climbed into her husband's new black Tesla. Not a sound could be heard as the car glided beneath a few streetlamps before leaving the neighborhood and disappearing into the dark.

In the wee hours of the morning, Officer Jack Trudeau responded to an alarm at the Hot Rocks Café. When he arrived, the front window lay scattered across the sidewalk. He inspected the glass on the café floor and confirmed the window was broken from the outside. June was nowhere to be seen. He recovered a torn piece of her checkered dress and bagged a curled plastic fragment from a sharp piece of glass protruding from the bottom of the window frame. A smash-and-run kidnapping. Good sense prevailed, though, and he reported the incident as a theft, not a kidnapping.

A brief search of traffic camera footage identified a suspect driving a black Tesla, but he lost the trail when the car turned off Main Street.

....

(Present)

At 6:00 a.m., Majorie parks her car in the back of Porter's Department Store and waits for a few minutes before a second vehicle pulls up beside her. Two women, dressed from head to toe in black, pull June from the trunk of Majorie's car and carry her to the building's back door. Marjorie steadies June against the wall of the building as her lifelong friend, Annabelle Porter, punches a code into the keypad, opens the door, and deactivates the alarm. June's right foot gets caught in the door as they enter, and the women struggle a bit before giving her a hard yank. Fortunately, the shoe is glued on, and she escapes with only a mild red paint smear on her black leather shoes.

Their plan is simple: return June to her pre-politics job as a lingerie model and let her live out her final days hiding in plain sight in the women's clothing department, dressed in lacy underwear and bra. But two problems arise once they strip her down. Her wig and shoes are glued on tight. Then there is the hack job Søren did in reattaching her right arm. The mangled arm has a bloody look from the red glue used to reattach it. June is clearly not suited to be a lingerie model anymore, and the ladies make an executive decision to reassign her to the outerwear department.

After some struggles redressing June, she ends up in the south corner dressed in a stylish rain jacket, holding an open umbrella instead of a Vote for Maggie sign with her permanently raised hand. The whole ordeal takes much longer than expected, and it's eight o'clock before they finish up—the store opens in an hour.

As the duo tidy up, Marjorie's phone rings. She recognizes her husband's ringtone and answers it.

"Marjorie, where are you, honey? I woke up, and you were gone."

"Just running a few errands, dear. I'll be home in no time. Don't worry, just fix yourself a little breakfast."

"The police called me thirty minutes ago, and I came downtown to identify my Tesla at the back of Porters. I also saw Annabelle's car there. I'm in front of the store right now with the police. Marjorie, we talked about this, and I asked you to put it behind you. Please tell me you didn't kidnap the mannequin again."

There is a long pause as Marjorie puts the phone on mute, scurries to the front of the store, and looks out the third-floor window to see Don, two police officers, and a growing crowd expectantly looking up at the building.

"Holy hell," she says, and Annabelle comes to have a look. She turns the phone off mute, "Darling, I can assure you there's nothing going on here. You and the police can go home. Everything is under control." She peeks out the window again and sees Don hand his phone to one of the policemen.

"Mrs. Wisely, this is Officer Jack Trudeau. I understand there's some bad blood between you and the mannequin, but if you come down, release the hostage—sorry, mannequin—and agree to pay for the broken window, I'm sure we can sort things out."

Marjorie blows a fuse. "Bad blood! Bad blood! She has no blood. She's nothing but an evil lump of plastic pretending to be the mayor. The only way this plastic bitch is coming down is the quick way." She ends the call.

Onlookers move back as the police clear the area. Marjorie scans the window and sees that because the building was constructed before air-conditioning, there are vent panels along each side. She pushes one open and figures there is enough room to squeeze a mannequin through. She hears voices drifting up from below.

"Look, someone is opening a window."

Hoodie Boy screams," No, she's going to defenestrate the mayor-elect."

Most of the crowd stares at Hoodie Boy, not catching his drift.

"She's going to assassinate her by throwing her out the window. Ever wonder why so many people opposing the Russian government end up jumping out of windows? And now poor innocent June Cleaver is about die the same way."

Marjorie has grabbed the umbrella out of June's hand, and, despite Annabelle's protestations, she pushes June's right arm and head through the open vent panel.

Officer Trudeau retrieves a bullhorn from his vehicle. "Ma'am. Do not, I repeat, do not throw the mannequin out the window. It will only make things worse."

Marjorie's head appears at the edge of the window, partially blocked by June's wig. "Poor, innocent June Cleaver! What kind of idiots are you? She can't be mayor. She's not a person—she doesn't have a brain. She's a useless piece of molded plastic. Get a grip, people."

"She outsmarted you the first time you kidnapped her," shouts Hoodie Boy.

The second police officer warns him to stay quiet. As the officer turns away, Hoodie Boy flips Marjorie the bird.

Her eyes narrow to slits, and June's left shoulder emerges, but her hand gets stuck on the inside edge of the window. Marjorie pushes June's butt as hard as she can and screams at Annabelle: "Push her by the feet. We've gotta get this slut out of here."

Annabelle complies with a mighty shove, and June rockets out the window as her left thumb pops off and bounces on the floor at Marjorie's feet.

A woman in the crowd screams, "Incoming, take cover."

June's limbs disarticulate on impact with the asphalt. Her torso bounces up, and her head shoots down Main Street, careening off a few car hoods in stopped traffic. Hoodie Boy rushes to retrieve it.

Nine blocks away, Melonie is unaware of the events unfolding at Porter's Department Store as she reads the headline "Mayor-elect June Cleaver Stolen Again." "Good riddance," she says under her breath and quickly looks around to make sure Thaddeus didn't hear her. Yesterday he said he was worried that she was taking the whole election saga too seriously, and she thinks he is probably right.

At ten in the morning, the city clerk's office declares Maggie the winner, stating that June was not old enough to be mayor; her registered manufacture date was twelve years ago. They also noted that June's head, presented to them by her unofficial campaign manager, was also ineligible to serve.

While the drama at Porter's Department Store raged, Søren recorded the entire debacle from June's perspective by activating the remaining camera in her head. The dramatic video ended when her head bounced into traffic, but he sent the unedited footage to North River News.

At six o'clock, Thaddeus and Melonie are transfixed by the video of June's last flight. Either Marjorie or Annabelle had pushed upward as June exited the window, causing her body to rotate head over foot. Every time her head looked up, the camera caught a stunning image of Marjorie leaning halfway out the window with her middle finger pressed to the bridge of her nose.

Connie Carter's closing comment on the segment was, "So there you have it, folks. Pastor Don Wisely's wife, Marjorie, delivers a final one-finger salute to former mayor-elect June Cleaver on her way out the window."

The Grotto

The excitement from the election subsided over the next six months. Maggie was turning out to be an exceptionally good mayor. Thaddeus thought she would be competent, but her flair for the job exceeded his expectations. She was instrumental in obtaining several state and federal grants to help with the North Bank Rehabilitation Project, which was several more than Mayor John had ever secured. Maggie also spent a couple of hours each day knocking on doors or visiting public venues to ask people how the city could improve its services. Her approval rating was over sixty percent, and, true to her promise, her monthly salary went directly to the food banks.

Melonie's deal with Blankers Real Estate had resulted in a significant cleanup of the old dump site, where they uncovered twenty-seven barrels of toxic waste and immediately had them properly disposed of. Melonie unofficially told Thaddeus that Carl Jr. was close to bankruptcy since his sister made him personally bankroll the entire cleanup. Although the source of the sludge remained unknown—all markings had been scrubbed off the barrels—the good news was Blankers Real Estate was building a quaint memorial park honoring the city's founder. They coordinated with Melonie's team to ensure work on the riverbank restoration and the park went smoothly.

Springtime at the botanical gardens was a sight to behold as new life arose from a winter slumber.

On a Wednesday afternoon, Thaddeus, busy in greenhouse 9, looked up to see Maud Mueller coming down the center aisle. Maud was the botanical garden's longest-standing patron. Thaddeus had once dug through some old records and found that Maud was on the original founding committee. She looked fresh and spry for her ninety-six years, dressed in her flowery green-and-white spring dress with a light yellow jacket. She held her walking stick like a military baton.

Technically, greenhouse 9 was off-limits to the public, but Thaddeus certainly wasn't going to argue the point. Even though he had walked with her many times on her weekly visits, he couldn't recall her ever entering this greenhouse.

"Maud, it is so good to see you. I hope you'll be dropping by this summer. I think I saw you here last week."

"Yes, last Wednesday was my first time back this season. But, God willing, I will be a regular again this year." She smacked the top of the table with her walking stick. "Your Japanese maple saplings are looking healthy." She picked one up to examine it and poked a finger into the moist soil. "You're going to need to get them in the ground soon."

"Yes, ma'am. I plan to put some of them in the northeast quadrant, near your property line."

Maud lived in a beautiful Victorian home next to the botanical gardens. Thaddeus knew the house was magnificent, but he considered the eighteen acres spread out in a wedge shape behind it to be the real treasure. Her property bordered the entire eastern edge of the botanical gardens and stretched down to the riverbank.

"You're doing a great job here, Thaddeus. I'm excited about the native ecological restoration you and Franky are planning. It's an excellent idea."

He looked up in surprise since an official public announcement had yet to happen. "So you've met Franky?"

"Yes, a wonderful man. I wandered down to the river bank last week and talked to him over the fence for about an hour."

Thaddeus pictured the overgrown, uneven terrain on Maud's side. "You walked all the way down there over that rough ground?"

Maud gave him a steely look. "I'm old, not dead, Thaddeus. I've been walking that property since I was a little girl." She smacked the planting table again with her walking stick for good measure.

He recalled a lawsuit from three years ago. A man tried to take her purse but ended up being coldcocked on the back of his head with that solid oak walking stick of hers. He was unconscious for three minutes, during which she zip-tied his right wrist to the lower frame of a shopping cart. He was gone when the police arrived, but they found him three blocks away, bent over the cart to accommodate his bound right hand and hobbling down the street, pushing the cart with his left hand. Subsequently, he sued her for assault but lost. The judge's parting comment to the courtroom urged Maud not to go so easy on him next time.

"Now, I have some business I want to discuss with you. So can you please offer an old lady a seat and a cup of tea?"

Thaddeus didn't know what to make of that statement, but he hustled off and retrieved his two fold-up lawn chairs. He set them up by the planting table, giving her the one without the broken straps, and rushed to get two cups of tea.

Once they were settled, Maud took a sip and contemplated the taste. "Very nice, Thaddeus. Chinese oolong tea, if I am not mistaken. What temperature do you steep it at?"

"I have a temperature-controlled water kettle that I set at one-hundred-and-ninety-five degrees Fahrenheit. Melonie likes it at the full two hundred and twelve degrees, but the slightly cooler temperature brings out a more subtle flavor, in my opinion."

"I must agree with you." She took another long sip before getting down to business. "I have a proposition I want to discuss with you. But before we get to that, I'll give you some unsolicited advice."

Thaddeus raised his eyebrows.

"I remember several times last summer when Melonie accompanied us on walks around the garden. She is a lovely woman. I also made some inquiries and discovered she is smart as a whip. Brains and beauty. It's a winning combination, Thaddeus, and I am old enough to recognize that you two have something special." She pointed her finger at him and slowly shook it as she stared him in the eye. "You need to marry that girl. If you let it go too long, she will move on. Life is short, and you must act decisively when the right opportunities arise."

Thaddeus had purchased a ring just a week ago and was going to collect it from the jeweler tomorrow before they went to the coast for a four-day mini vacation. "I'm one step ahead of you, Maud. Just between you and me, I am proposing to her this weekend."

Maud pulled a handkerchief from her jacket pocket and dabbed the corner of her eye. "Don't pay any attention to me. I'm just a sentimental gal."

She took a moment to recover before continuing. "What I am really here to talk about is my property, which has been in our family forever. Hell, in four more years, I will have been in my house for a hundred years. Mr. Mueller, God rest his soul, was a good husband, but we could never have any children. I'm the last of my line. I won't live forever, and I want to ensure our riverfront property becomes a legacy for all the people in North River. I want it to be an extension of the botanical gardens. The problem is most of the politicians and bureaucrats in this town are functional idiots. I don't think our new mayor is, but she will be replaced soon enough. I need a person with vision, integrity, and creativity to ensure my family's legacy is properly cared for. Thaddeus, you are that person. I'm in the process of finalizing the transfer of sixteen of my eighteen acres to the city to be part of the botanical gardens. The arrangement will hold the land in a trust, and I want you to be the trustee. Nothing happens unless you approve it. By the way, you just spilled tea on your trousers."

Thaddeus's life equation was rearranging itself in a most mysterious and shocking way. He knew to expect the unexpected, but the magnitude of Maud's plans overwhelmed him mid-sip, allowing tea to dribble down his mug and splatter on his pants.

Her proposal for the botanical gardens left him speechless, so Maud continued. "I know it's a lot to spring on you, but I want the North River Botanical Gardens to be one of the best in the country. But it needs someone of your caliber to make that happen. Now, I know that my vision requires considerable funding. But I wasn't willing to sell a single acre to those damn greedy developers who come knocking at my door. So, for the past three years, I've been lobbying like-minded people to establish a trust fund for the new extension. Our funding is sound, and I hope you'll say yes to what I'm offering."

Thaddeus had regained his wits. "My answer is an unequivocal yes. It would be the honor of a lifetime to oversee the expansion. I already have ideas."

"I'm sure you do. Don't think for a minute that I haven't seen you standing by the fence daydreaming about that undeveloped section of the riverbank."

Thaddeus found himself blushing like someone had read his innermost thoughts.

Maud took a long slow sip of tea. "Good. Now that we've settled that, I have another piece of business. I am packing my bags soon and moving to that new retirement home in the West Hill district. I have rattled around in that big house of mine for too long. Life goes forward, not backward, Thaddeus. But don't worry, as long as I can drag myself out of bed in the morning, I will be taking my weekly stroll through the gardens with you. But I'm rambling on. The issue at hand is I want to sell my home and the remaining two acres to you and Melonie. I have a feeling there will soon be kids running around. They'll need a big backyard to play in."

Thaddeus was at a loss for words for the second time that day. He and Melonie had been lightly following the housing market, so he was aware of the approximate value of two acres and a Victorian home in the center of town.

"Since the land gift to the city is part of my legacy, I want to ensure it gets the attention it deserves. You need to be living close to the expansion of the Botanical Gardens, and my home is the best place to do that. I will sell it to you at half the market value. I know that is still a lot of money.

But being a nosy woman with connections, I also know you are doing quite well with your recent patents, and Melonie is old enough to draw from her trust fund."

Thaddeus wondered why he was always the last to know things. A trust fund? Since money was a minor part of his life equation, he had never asked Melonie about her finances. He just assumed she saved a bit from her paycheck like everyone else. Even when they discussed financing a house, she simply said she was sure they could come up with a reasonable down payment and that their two salaries could cover a mortgage.

"Maud, you know that the closer I live to these gardens, the happier I will be. But Melonie has to be on board too. First, let me convince her to marry me, and then we can talk about the house."

Maud gave him her nicest smile and finished her tea.

"Next Wednesday at two in the afternoon, you two come by my house. One look inside, and Melonie will say yes." She rose and set off down the center aisle with her walking stick tucked under her arm like a swagger stick.

Thaddeus proposed on a nearly deserted beach at sunset. The only setback was when he produced the ring. His nervous fingertips fumbled a bit, and the gold and diamond disappeared under an incoming wave. But after a frantic search, he retrieved it, and Melonie said yes.

At 2:00 p.m. Wednesday, they knocked on Maud's front door.

After a cup of tea, she shooed Thaddeus out of the house. "I know you're already on board, Thaddeus. Melonie and I are going to tour the house alone—we don't need your opinions distracting us from the task at hand. You go out back and find Joseph. I don't believe I mentioned it the other day, but I expect that you'll allow Joseph to continue renting the groundskeeper cottage."

Maud's approach to life was one of unabashed confidence mixed with a healthy dose of authoritarianism. As far as she was concerned, the sale was a done deal.

Melonie raised her eyebrows, but Thaddeus nodded as the pieces clicked into place. He had often observed a man doing work around Maud's property but had always assumed he was a contracted landscaper. Joseph lived on the property, accounting for why Thaddeus had observed him hard at work when daily contractors would normally have knocked off and gone home.

"If Joseph isn't home, you may find him at the grotto just down the hill from the cottage. He likes to meditate there."

Thaddeus stopped at the back door. "Do you actually have a grotto on the property?"

"I think I just said so, Thaddeus. Grandfather built it in the late 1800s. He was convinced he had to have one when he returned from a European trip. Evidently, they were all the rage there. But you'll see it's in need of some repair."

"Is it a purely artificial cave, or is it built on a natural feature?"

"He claimed there was already a small cave there, and he expanded it into a grotto. But go look for yourself," she said, waving him out the door.

Thaddeus knocked on the door of the stone cottage but got no answer. He spent a few minutes examining the sandstone, running his hands over the intricate, hand-carved door and window frames. Behind the house, he descended a small set of stairs cut into the native stone. He rounded a sharp bend to the right and found himself on the floor of the grotto, admiring tilework that looked like Roman mosaic flooring. The grotto extended to his right beneath a sandstone overhang, leaving the area to his left exposed to the sky. Water trickled down a massive mosaic wall in the back of the grotto and then flowed into a sinuous stream that crossed the floor and fed into a small reflection pool at the far edge, overlooking the river.

Joseph sat cross-legged on a stone dais deep inside the grotto and turned to Thaddeus. With a tiny smile, he motioned for Thaddeus to come over. His long black hair, lightly streaked with strands of gray, was tied in a neat braid that fell between his shoulder blades.

Thaddeus took his time observing the extraordinary details of the grotto.

Joseph walked over to a teapot sitting on a propane camping stove. He poured Thaddeus a warm cup and gestured toward a bench carved into the sandstone wall. "Thaddeus, it's a pleasure to meet you. I'm Joseph. Your gardening fame precedes you, thanks to Maud. I understand you're going to be the property's new owner."

"Well, my fiancée, Melonie, and I are thinking about buying the house plus two acres. But nothing is finalized."

"Where is Melonie?"

"She and Maud are having a walk around the house."

"In that case, you are the new owners. Maud is a force of nature and will not be denied. Before you leave today, Melonie will fall in love with the place and insist you two buy the house."

Thaddeus absorbed the comment and turned his attention to the view of the river. Life was on the move, and his equation was rapidly shifting. There was something about Joseph that he liked, and Thaddeus was not one to ignore his instincts.

"I trust you'll continue to rent the groundskeeper's cottage?" asked

Thaddeus.

"Yes, I'd like to. It's an architectural gem."

"The exterior is in pristine condition. I presume you are the one who restored it."

Joseph nodded.

"What do you know about the construction of this grotto?"

"Maud told me what her grandfather told her. But there are some things that don't add up. A close look suggests that there was a sizable natural cave here before the grotto. Maybe we'll investigate once you move in."

Joseph led him down the slope from the grotto and showed him the structural remains of what used to be extensive gardens close to the river. Thaddeus had never suspected it, but below the overgrowth were partially buried stone terraces and stairs providing firm evidence. Careful excavation would be the first order of business.

He returned to the house after two hours and found Melonie and Maud sitting in wicker rockers on the front porch, chatting like family. He reflected on Joseph's comments as he and Melonie descended the stairs. As the front door shut, Melonie stopped, looked him in the eye, and said, "We are buying this house." Thaddeus understood this was not a question.

....

(Present – Autumn)

Thaddeus and Joseph stand at the riverside edge of the grotto by the reflection pond, gazing at the whitish-gray back wall of the cave. Behind them are signs of the first riverside excavations. Next summer, the expansion of the North River Botanical Gardens will begin.

A crisp October wind and sunny blue skies portend the arrival of autumn when the gardens of North River prepare for their descent into winter. Maud's house was purchased at the beginning of July, and the past three months were a whirlwind of moving-in activity. Thaddeus also had the area surveyed to ensure the grotto was firmly on his side of the property line, not part of the land gifted to the city.

"Where have you stored the tiles?" asks Thaddeus.

"In the workroom at the back of my cottage. The project took three weeks, but they were all removed intact from the back wall. Everything is cataloged for an easy reconstruction of the original mosaic if that's what we decide to do."

A power cord snakes down the stone stairs from an external outlet at

Joseph's cottage. Plugged into the end of the cord is a rock saw with a twelve-inch blade.

Joseph looks at Thaddeus and asks, "Do you want to do the honors?"

"In case we make a mess of things, I should definitely be the one to make the first cuts."

Thaddeus puts on his protective gear, picks up the saw, and moves closer to the back wall. When Joseph removed the tiles, his work revealed a solid layer of cement. Thaddeus makes four cuts, then takes a crowbar and pops off a square of cement, exposing a brick wall.

After an hour of careful cutting, they have a substantial window with a cool, damp breeze flowing out from the darkness. Joseph hands Thaddeus a flashlight, and he takes a peek inside.

"Holy crap! We aren't talking about a crevasse in the rock—this is a big cave."

Enlarging the opening so the men can fit through takes another four hours. While Joseph goes to retrieve another flashlight, Thaddeus steps through the opening they have made and drops down about a foot. His feet are submerged in water up to his knees. The natural cave is roughly eight feet across and seven feet high, with a center drainage canal carved into the stone floor. A small stream empties from the canal into the basin where Thaddeus stands. Water from the basin flows through a pipe leading to the grotto stream outside, and an overflow drain is visible to his left. The structure is well engineered.

Thaddeus finds a dry ledge beside the receiving pond and warns Joseph about the wet entry as he steps through. They work their way into the cave until it widens with a slightly higher ceiling. Neither Thaddeus nor Joseph can discern if the bigger chamber is natural or man-made, but they both notice the raised platform on the west wall with rotting wood planks on top.

Joseph slips back through the entrance hole and returns with a crowbar.

A puff of dust swirls upward as they pop off the rotting planks. But when everything settles, there is no question that the platform is a tomb and the skeleton inside is human.

... End ...

Rand Soler is a writer and artist living in the American Pacific Northwest. His work explores the intersection of art, science, and life on this small orb we call Earth, a backwater planet in the Orion Arm of the Milky Way Galaxy. Between his writing gigs, he works with fusion art, melding together painting, digital art, and photography.

Themes in Rand's work range from exploring the nature of sapient life in soft science fiction to reveling in the delightfully human eccentricities that make us each unique people. He often co-authors with Y.A. Picker.

Acknowledgments

Thanks to Y.A. Picker for his help and suggestions with the book and artwork.

Thanks to Lisa Kaitz for an excellent job copy editing the manuscript.